THE
LOVE
POTION

THE
LOVE
POTION

•

Ludima Gus Burton

AVALON BOOKS
NEW YORK

PRINTED IN THE UNITED STATES OF AMERICA
ON ACID-FREE PAPER
BY HADDON CRAFTSMEN, BLOOMSBURG, PENNSYLVANIA

To Erin Cartwright,
my helpful editor

Chapter One

"This powder will make a man fall in love with you. CAUTION: THROW ONLY A PINCH ON HIM."

The crystal bottle, filled with a glimmering white powder, felt smooth in Starr Evans' hand. She placed it on the rough stone railing of the balcony of her second-floor hotel suite. The love potion had been purchased on a whim. She didn't believe in magic. Yet, tonight, how she wished it were possible!

Loneliness wrapped around her heart.

She wanted a man to fall in love with her, to have a home and a family. But not by the mystic power of a love potion!

She yearned to be cherished for herself. Hun-

1

gered to be with one man forever—eat endless meals together and share thoughts and troubles. Someone she could be with and not watch every word. Someone who would share a deep and abiding love with her.

One man, always. And a love nothing could destroy.

Such a man didn't exist in the small mountain village of Rural Springs, New York. Once she thought she had found him. But his words meant nothing. They weren't backed by actions and commitment—commitment such as, I love you, will you marry me, live with only me, forever and ever?

Besides, The Featherstone Inn, her home with her aunt for the past three years, catered to honeymooners. Hardly the place for finding eligible bachelors.

She leaned over the railing of the wide ledge to look down at the main patio.

Soft lights bordered the Inn's pathways, highlighting the masses of daffodils, crocuses, and tulips. The fragrant breeze ruffled the new green leaves of the maple trees. It was an unusually mild evening in May. A perfect night for romance. Yet, no loving couples strolled through the gardens or danced cheek to cheek to the haunting love songs from the Twilight Bar.

Reaching for the potion, Starr turned to go back into her room. But her wandering thoughts made her careless. The bottle slipped from her hand. It rolled to the edge of the railing. The stopper fell out and crashed to the flagstones below.

Freed from its crystal abode, the shimmering powder cascaded like a sparkling waterfall to silver the hair and shoulders of a man who had stepped out onto the patio.

"What the devil . . . ?" The surprise in his deep voice was no less than what Starr felt, watching him brush the powder from his face.

"Oh, I'm so sorry," she called down to him. "The powder is harmless. Oh, my . . ." He looked a sight with powder flying around him in a cloud. She smothered the urge to laugh out loud.

"I'll be right down to help dust it off."

Before she turned to leave she saw the man clamp his lips together as if to cut off a retort. The frown on his forehead deepened.

Starr stepped back out of his sight. Great. Through her carelessness she'd upset her aunt's hotel guest—an attractive man at that. She left her suite hoping to placate, somehow, the irritated guest.

"So sorry about this," Starr said as she approached him few minutes later. "Let's see what I can do."

She tipped back her head to look up at the tall stranger. Unexpectedly, her breath caught in her throat and her heart rate quickened. She was aware of the luminous glow about him, the width of his powerful shoulders, and the warmth of his muscular body so close to her. The scent of spicy after-shave filled her nostrils. With effort, she took a deep breath and assessed the damage.

Though he had shaken his head vigorously and much of the powder had drifted away, what had once been black hair resembled a glittering snowball. A scowl drew his heavy eyebrows together over a fine patrician nose. His full, sensuous lips were pursed to a thin line.

"What is this stuff?" he demanded, his voice low, husky, and vibrating with suppressed feeling.

"I accidently tipped a bottle of powder over the railing. Here, let me . . ."

Raising on tiptoe, Starr reached up to flick the dust from his hair and met the intense and disturbing gaze of his narrowed blue eyes. Her hand stopped short of its target.

"You can shampoo your hair," she said, finding it hard to speak. Standing so close to him, she felt his male magnetism drawing her to him. She could have sworn it swept down her spine to curl her toes!

With difficulty she turned her attention to the

jacket. The shimmering powder lay all over it. How could there be so much from such a small bottle? Feeling shy and uncertain, her hands touched the broad shoulders of his navy blue suit coat. She hoped he wouldn't see how they trembled.

Starr brushed hard, then harder, to dislodge the powder. ". . . Have it cleaned off in a minute," she mumbled. Particles flew in every direction, making her cough and then sneeze.

"Stop. You're not helping."

Eric Hammond looked into the face of a woman whose high cheekbones hinted at Native American ancestry. Her large green eyes seemed to pull him in like a man caught in quicksand. Full lips tempted him to cover them with his. Some of the shimmering powder had settled on her dark golden hair and tawny eyelashes. It warred with the freckles sprinkled across her cheeks and pert nose.

Lightly, he brushed the glitter away from the velvety skin of her cheeks. It silvered the ends of his fingers. Smooth and silky, just like her cheek.

He stepped back, needing to put distance between them. "What is this? A new bath product?"

"Definitely not. It's something I bought at my friend Glenda's New Age Store. It's supposed to be . . . it's—it's just supposed to look pretty in a crystal bottle."

Lowering her gaze, she tried once more to brush his shoulders. He stopped her by taking her hands in his large ones, causing Starr to confess, "It doesn't want to come off. I'll have your coat cleaned."

Moving away a pace, she introduced herself, "I'm Starr Evans."

"Star?"

"Spelled with two R's. My mother was a devotee of astrology at the time of my birth."

"Interesting name." His gaze skimmed over her. "It suits you. I'm Eric Hammond." He looked into her eyes. "Are you a guest also?"

"I live here with my aunt who owns and runs this Inn." She added, "I also work part-time—waitress, desk clerk, chambermaid, and accountant. Whatever. To help out." She slanted a quick look at him. "How long are you and your wife staying?"

"I'm not married. Now or ever."

Relief filled Starr. At least she hadn't dumped a love potion on a married man. What unthinkable complications might have been the result—if the love potion was real! Still, it was unusual for a lone male, one opposed to marriage, to register at their well-known honeymoon resort. It had never happened before in her memory. Curiosity got the better of her.

"Ah . . . have you had a chance to read the Inn's brochure?" At his negative nod, Starr explained, "We make reservations mainly for honeymoon couples."

"Honeymooners?" A wide smile softened the hard planes of his face and made him less formidable. He gave a low chuckle. "The desk clerk did act confused and had trouble registering me."

Starr groaned. "That must have been Bethany, our new clerk."

"Is there a problem with my staying here? It's close to Bradley Laboratory where I'll be working as a visiting cancer research consultant."

"I—I guess it'll be all right. That is, if you don't feel uncomfortable among so many newly-weds."

Eric shrugged his shoulders. The white powder swirled around him. "I'll be fine. My work keeps me fully occupied."

"If you'll give me your jacket . . ."

He stared at her for what felt like an eternity— as if he saw her as a speciman under his microscope. He slipped off the coat and handed it to her.

"You'll have the jacket back by dinner tomorrow, Mr. Hammond."

"Eric."

"Eric." Her gaze shifted to his head. "The powder should come out of your hair. I apologize again for my clumsiness. Good night." Starr turned away and walked up the wide central stairs to her suite.

Eric watched until she disappeared around the curve of the stairs. She had left behind a haunting, flowery fragrance that made him want to follow her.

He shook his head at his errant thoughts. He walked briskly to the elevator. He ignored the raised eyebrows and giggles of the young couple who exited.

As Starr dressed in the morning, her thoughts returned often to Eric Hammond. Laughter bubbled from her. Some pinch! She had dumped a whole bottle on him. So much for following directions.

Magic dust—if she was to believe the bottle. Starr gave a little groan. Why had she succumbed to her best friend Glenda's sales pitch about her new acquisition? Every time she went to the New Age Store, Glenda had something different to show her. No matter how much Starr argued with her and stated she was a rank disbeliever, Glenda managed to put that little doubt in her mind. What if there was some little-bitty truth to her story?

Dissatisfaction with her life weighed on Starr's heart. Her dream of falling in love with the right man seemed further and further away from attainment. A small part of her wanted to believe in Glenda's crystals and charms, but her common sense prevailed. Magic wasn't going to dictate her love life.

Yesterday she had said to Glenda, "I'll buy this beautiful crystal bottle, but I don't swallow your story that it's filled with a love potion. When one of your other customers uses it and gets her man, then I might become a believer."

Eric Hammond.

Any woman would consider him a worthy candidate for the love potion—lean, powerfully built, with the broad shoulders of a football player and the slim hips of a track star. Last night his Irish-blue eyes, deep-set and intense, appeared to look into her soul.

After glancing at her watch, Starr rushed to finish dressing. She took the stairs to the lobby of the Inn. She needed to get to Evans Specialties, a company she had started three years ago. She designed and printed travel brochures. A customer had been promised the flyers on Rome this morning by eleven.

"Starr." Aunt Maud stopped Starr's approach to the exit. "Do you have time to take these towels to Room 302? And there's some complaint about lost luggage."

Starr always made time for her aunt's requests for help. "Of course. No problem."

Standing outside Room 302 a few minutes later, she balanced the stack of towels under her chin. "Housekeeping," she called after knocking on the door.

She knocked again and realized she didn't know the name of the guest.

The door jerked open. It swung wide.

"Oh, my gracious!"

Eric Hammond stood in the doorway. A large bath towel around his shoulders caught the water dripping off his hair. Black jeans hugged his trim, hard body, and his feet were bare.

"Look at me," he commanded in a furious voice.

Starr gulped, feeling as though the breath had been knocked out of her. "I'm looking, I'm look-ing," she whispered, letting her gaze wander over him.

"Look at my hair, my hair!"

Silver flakes snared every strand of black hair. They glittered in the overhead light.

"Oh, my, you look like a Christmas ornament!" She almost dropped the towels.

"Tell me what to do. The powder washed out but the glitter won't budge. Got any practical ideas, Ms. Evans, besides bringing me more towels?"

Starr controlled an urge to laugh at the sight he presented. Furthermore, Eric Hammond didn't act like a man in love. So much for the power of store-bought love potions.

Tipping back her head, she studied him. "Maybe I can comb out the glitter." After putting down the towels, she pulled out a chair from the desk. "Please sit down."

"Try it. This is my first day at Bradley Laboratory as a consultant. I can't go looking like this."

Standing behind his towel-covered shoulders, Starr breathed in the aroma of his spicy aftershave, squelching the urge to caress his smooth strong jaw. Instead, she threaded her fingers through the crisp locks, mesmerized by the silver flakes playing hide-and-seek. They were like quicksilver. None could be captured between her fingertips. She drew in a deep, shuddering breath. Such beautiful hair to touch.

"Don't you want to use my comb now?"

Though resenting his understandable sarcasm,

Starr took the comb. She began to pull it through his hair. The comb snagged on a tangle.

"Take it easy."

"Sorry." She worked in silence, his soft hair entwined around her fingers. Heat like an electric current traveled from her fingertips and into her body. It threatened her concentration. Ignoring her reaction as best she could, Starr continued her efforts.

And nothing changed.

The silver flakes persisted in their game. They teased her. One minute it looked as though they were gone, and then—bang!—they were back as bright as ever. Not one shiny flake fell to the towel.

A groan escaped her.

"Not having any success, Ms. Evans?"

Defeated in her efforts, Starr tossed the comb on the dresser. "No, Mr. Hammond."

"You got me into this and you better come up with a solution. I can't go to work looking like a light bulb."

Starr checked her wristwatch. She gasped, "I'm sorry, but I can't stay any longer. I have to get to my office. Keep washing your hair. The powder came out. So will the glitter."

She headed toward the door.

"Wait," Eric called. "What about my brief-case?"

"What briefcase?"

"It's not with my luggage, and I need it."

Starr's moan came from deep within. What else could happen to this guest at their normally well-run hotel? "What did it look like?"

"It's dark brown cowhide with wide straps and contains critical research papers. I saw my luggage and briefcase loaded into your van."

"Did you have a name tag on it?"

"Of course."

"I'll get to it right away. Again, I'm sorry you're having such a bad time with us." She turned to leave once more.

Before she took a step, Eric lightly put his hands on her shoulders and turned her toward him. He brought his face close to hers. His breath was warm against her lips. For a heart-stopping moment, she thought he was going to kiss her.

"You're leaving me with my hair like this?"

"I–I guess so. I'll go to the store where I bought the stuff and find out more about it. My only other suggestion is for you to cover your head with something."

While he glared at her, Starr slipped from his grasp. She ran out the door.

She grimaced at the sound of the door slamming. *Temper, temper, Eric!* But she did wish he'd kissed her until she was breathless.

Head cover. A hat. Yes, of course.

She spotted one of the college student waiters.

"Allen, would you run an errand for me? I'll clear it with Aunt Maud. Go to Grimes Department Store and buy a New York Yankees baseball cap. Deliver it to Mr. Hammond in Room 302. Have it put on my account. Thanks."

"Is Mr. Hammond a Yankees fan?"

"He is now."

Having solved one of Eric's problems, Starr went to the baggage room. No briefcase. When she questioned the porter he remembered taking only one piece of luggage to Mr. Hammond's room. A search of the van proved fruitless. Starr sighed. It must have been placed in another guest's room.

"Gretchen, I've a job for you. Please check with the guests who came yesterday. Find out if they have Eric Hammond's briefcase." She gave her a description of it. "Call me at my office if it's located."

"Will do, Starr."

"Thanks. I'm out of here."

While Starr worked to get caught up on her orders, thoughts of Eric Hammond haunted her all day. Could he become her dream Mr. Right? At least, he fit the picture. Tall, dark, handsome, unmarried. That bright glow around him from the glitter made him resemble Prince Charming as painted in her old book of fairy tales.

If the real inner man didn't measure up to her expectations, external attributes counted for little. She knew nothing about Eric's inner man. If he stayed in town for any length of time, she might find out.

Last night and this morning he had smiled only once. Her first reaction to his predicament was to laugh. Had he no sense of humor at all? A shudder went through her. No way did she want a morose, grim man. But maybe events in his life and his profession made him serious. What would it take to make him smile—easily? Laugh—hilariously?

Starr's hands lay idle on her keyboard. All too soon she was going to be thirty years old, with her biological clock ticking away. She longed for at least one child, a home, and a loving husband to cuddle up next to every night. But did she want to open her life to another rejection?

Bitter bile rose to her throat. She had had a painful experience. She had given her all, only to have lies and infidelity tear her trust to shreds. Words of love had been only empty sounds. Dare she trust her heart to a man again?

She wanted to dismiss the notion that a pinch of a love potion could make a man fall in love with her. Yet the idea grabbed her imagination and tantalized her.

She mocked herself. No way did she believe in this mad magic, nor did she want a man under those conditions. He had to love her—body and soul, heart and mind—for herself alone. Also it had to be his idea, not something brought on by a white powder in a bottle.

At odd moments, during the day, when she least expected it, Starr found herself giggling.

She kept picturing Eric's sparkling hair. He belonged in a Midsummer Night's Eve costume ball. She could imagine him in a black velvet jacket with gold buttons and fringed epaulets, his glittering hair giving him a halo of majesty. Eye-catching tan tights molded his firm thighs, and black leather boots came up to his knees. And, of course, gossamer wings! Laughter bubbled up again.

Did he wear the Yankees baseball cap with his business suit today? Sobering, she realized this might not be so funny.

How had his new colleagues reacted to his appearance? Starr groaned. She hoped the stars, for which she was named, would be with him, and that he had been able to come up with a believable explanation to save his dignity.

After closing her office that afternoon, Starr walked down Main Street. She stopped to look at a mint-green sundress in the window of Edna's Boutique; she'd buy it tomorrow. She had to hurry to the Midtown Cleaners before it closed.

"What? How much?" Her shriek bounced off the walls of the small cleaning store. "What did you do, Stanley, clean it with a gold solution?"

"Starr, I had such a hard time cleaning the dark jacket. Those silver sparkles! It took four cleanings."

Starr paid the bill and arranged to have the jacket delivered to Eric's room before dinner.

A hard mass settled in the pit of her stomach. If harsh cleaning solutions had to be used on the coat, would water and gentle shampoo ever work on Eric's hair? She groaned. Glenda was now her only hope. Her New Age knowledge and expertise were to be tested.

By the time the sign of the New Age Store, swinging back and forth from the black wrought-iron bracket, came into view, Starr had worked herself into a mini-frenzy of worry. The brass bells at the top of the door threatened to fall to the floor because she banged the door shut.

"You and your new products!" she told Glenda. "I'm in a pack of trouble, and you have to help me. What was in that bottle?"

"Ah, you've followed the instructions and—"

"Followed the instructions? No, I dumped the whole bottle on a stranger. Now Eric Hammond, a paying hotel guest, can't get it out of his hair. He's very upset."

"The—the whole bottle? What were you thinking? The directions said only a pinch."

"Believe me, I didn't do it deliberately. It was an accident."

Glenda nodded and adjusted on her forehead the black band with a big red stone in the middle of it. Her long silver earrings swung from side to side. A saffron silk caftan flowed from her shoulders. A costume to suit her store, thought Starr.

She drew Starr into her back room and nudged her into the comfortable armchair before handing her a cup of herbal tea.

"Relax, and tell me what happened. Honestly, Starr, why can't you ever follow directions?"

"Don't put the blame on me. How was I to know it wasn't a good idea to put the bottle on my railing?"

Starr briefly related what had happened. She giggled. "You should see him. A disco ball has nothing on him."

"Well, you did pour the whole bottle on him."

Starr glared at her friend. "Not on purpose." She put her cup on the table with a clatter. "Why couldn't you have sold me a bottle without glitter? The plain powder washed out with no problem. Who did you buy this from?"

"I never saw her before. Just another traveling salesperson. She was waiting for me to open up. A funny little woman wearing a black cape and a crazy straw hat covered with real flowers. She smelled just wonderful."

"What did she say?"

"Something like, 'Dearie me, you must be very careful with these.' She pointed to the directions on the bottle. She even made me read them aloud twice. She insisted I buy all six bottles. Her price was reasonable, and I felt sorry for the poor thing." Glenda rolled her eyes. "You know I'm a sucker for this kind of a thing. Right up my alley. A great sales pitch!"

Glenda searched her desk drawer. "Here's her card. Samantha Charms, Astral Industries. Hmm, there's no address or phone number. Some cute flower designs, though." Glenda turned the card over and read the scribbled message. "'I'll be back in three months.'"

"Three months!" Starr held her aching head between her hands. "If we don't find some way to get the glitter out of Eric's hair, the hotel could be in legal trouble."

"What's this Eric like—besides looking like an ornament and being mad as a bull? Could he be the answer to your dreams?"

"Dark and handsome, in a grim way. He didn't see the humor in the accident at all. Thirty-ish. A consultant at Bradley Laboratory."

Glenda took another sip of her tea. Suddenly, she sat up straight. "Your aunt's honeymoon hotel! Heavens, don't tell me you dumped the potion on a happily married man! Talk about complications—just in case this is the real thing."

"He's not married—'now or ever' were his exact words."

"A confirmed bachelor, eh? Wonder what woman done him wrong?"

Starr shrugged her shoulders. "I'd guess he's the one who pushes women away. He wasn't very friendly last night." Starr refilled her cup. "What are we going to do about his hair?"

"You'll think of something. You always do."

Starr stood up and began to pace up and down. "Let's look at the other five bottles."

"I've put them away. A good Christmas item." She hurried to get them.

The bottles were artistic creations. They were identical to the one Starr had purchased—with one exception. There wasn't a speck of glitter in their white powder.

Starr looked at Glenda and a chill crawled up her spine. This was weird. Was hers a special bottle? She shook her head. "I refuse to believe there's magic here. It's plain ordinary glitter, and for reasons I can't logically explain, it likes Eric's hair." The sigh she exhaled came from the depths of her being. "When I go home, I hope I don't run into him. He may become my dream man tomorrow, but tonight he'll be my nightmare."

Her nightmare was waiting for her in the lobby.

The Yankees baseball cap sat firmly on his head. He wore the same black jeans he'd worn that morning, but he'd added a sweatshirt with the Yankees logo. Even with the scowl, the classic beauty of his face set her senses into a tailspin. Her attraction to him made her heart race and caused her blood to heat in an unexpected way.

"There you are." Eric walked up to within a foot of her.

Starr gave him her full attention.

"What have you learned? Can your shopkeeper get rid of this pesky stuff?" he asked.

Starr shook her head. "Unfortunately, she can't get any additional information for . . . uh . . . three months."

"Three months!" His shout had all heads in the lobby turning in their direction. He glared down at her. "Three months of eating in a diner because of the dress code in the Inn's dining room? Three months of wearing this hat and having people gawking at me? No way!"

Eric reached out and pulled her close to him. Lowering his head he stared at her, nose to nose. Her limpid, enticing green eyes which locked with his made his head reel. His lips were a breath away from hers. He stopped just in time from yielding to the temptation her rosy mouth was offering him. With a great effort, he wrenched his hands from her shoulders and stepped away.

Why was he drawn to a woman who was disrupting his orderly existence? Why did she make his head spin every time she came around? He had no time for her. He didn't want this woman or any woman in his life. His work demanded total concentration, and that was the way he wanted it.

"You expect me to be a blasted freak for three months?"

"Nooo. We'll remove the glitter. I'm sure there's a simple remedy. You can use this one tonight."

He looked into the brown grocery bag Starr thrust at him. Two small bottles of liquid soap and vinegar, a half dozen eggs, a small bowl, and a whisk made no sense to him.

"You want me to cook?"

"Try this old remedy for hair problems. It's an egg shampoo. Here's what you do." Starr gave him the directions. Her smile danced like sunlight over him. "It'll work. I guarantee it."

"I'll try any fool idea at this point. But why the three-month wait for information?"

"The saleswoman . . ." Starr searched for an answer. ". . . has—has had to leave the country."

"Wise woman. I'd take myself out of reach, too."

Eric started to walk away. He turned back. "I'll make this egg shampoo, but I don't have any faith in old-fashioned, untested remedies. In the meantime, I'm going to do what I should have done before. I'll have the powder and glitter analyzed. Please bring the bottle to me by nine tomorrow morning, without fail."

He took several steps away from her, then stopped. He came back to stand close to her.

Her breath caught in her throat. The heat from his body reached her. His physical effect on her was so disturbing.

"I hope my briefcase has been found," he said. "I need my papers."

"I'm sorry, no." She cleared her throat of an

irritating tickle. "We think it was delivered to another guest. Unfortunately, we have to wait to question two couples. They went on a short trip. I'll make it my first priority in the morning."

"Please do and don't forget my sample." This time he strode rapidly to the elevator.

Starr stayed rooted to the spot long after Eric left. How was she going to tell him there was nothing to analyze? He was going to be upset. She had washed the bottle that morning.

Chapter Two

"What do you mean there isn't any powder for me to analyze? Where's the bottle? I know I can get a sample."

"I washed the bottle," Starr confessed in a low mumble, the next morning in his room.

"You what? You–you–you—! First you dump this stuff on me, and then you wash away the evidence?"

She cringed as his roar of exasperated rage filled the room.

Eric stood over her like an avenging giant. She gazed in his dark blue eyes. With a bewildered gasp she moved away from him. She hoped shiv-

ers of excitement were making him equally un-
nerved. His words killed her hope.

"Look at my hair. The egg shampoo didn't
work."

The glitter in his hair winked and shimmered.

"You glow brighter than a light bulb this morning," she said, holding in a desire to laugh hilariously.

"I know, I've seen myself." He glared at her in
disgust. "You're responsible for this. Suggest—
do—something."

Remorse filled her. He was so angry. Clearly at
his wit's end. Irrationally, she wanted to hug and
kiss him and make it all go away.

"Why don't you sit down? I'll comb your hair
again. I'll try to shake enough of the glitter onto
a sheet of paper for you to test." From the drawer
of the desk she took some hotel stationery. He did
as she asked, grumbling every inch of the way.

Her fingers ran along the soft, black strands of
hair. She tousled, pulled, and combed, but the glitter eluded her efforts.

Nothing. Not a sliver of silver fell to the paper.

While she struggled to get her sample, Eric endured slow torture because her spring flower fragrance tantalized him. Her hands, wrestling with
his hair, were setting him on fire. Why wasn't he

irritated with her instead of being captivated by her attractions?

This vexing female gave his hair a hard yank. "Hey, watch it! Did you get any?"

"No."

He stood up. "There's no use trying any longer. The stuff's there to stay for now. Don't suppose you have any more ideas?" He stared at her, waiting. "Thought not." He placed a Dodgers cap on his head. "I have to leave for work, looking like a rabid baseball fan."

She stared at Eric's attire. He had changed teams. A T-shirt with the Dodgers logo had joined the one on the cap. On his feet were white Michael Jordan sneakers.

She grinned. "You must be making a fashion statement at the lab. What explanation did you give?"

"Said I worked better when I was comfortable. They didn't approve—especially when the cap stayed on. They put it down to eccentricity. Can I hope I won't have to play the fool much longer?"

"Shampoo it some more. It seems to me that even though the glitter isn't washing completely out, it is getting dull." Walking toward the door, she explained, "I have to get to work myself."

"Have you found my briefcase? I can't have it fall into the hands of the wrong people."

"We've searched every room. We're still waiting for the return of some guests. One of them may have taken it in their car."

"It's imperative I get it back as soon as possible."

"We'll find it."

Eric stared at her for a moment before adjusting his cap. The opening at the back barely revealed the shining hair.

"What do you do, Starr?"

"I have my own business." He probably thought she was capable of only clerking in a small boutique. She thrust her chin into the air. "I print advertising brochures for travel agencies."

"A family business?"

"No. I worked for a travel agency after college and wanted to get out on my own. Since I like the field of advertising, designing and printing brochures was the way to go." Pride underscored her next words. "Business is booming."

"Your aunt runs this hotel. Is she married?"

"No. Aunt Maud's often teased because she has made the Inn such a well-known resort for honeymooners. She just tells them her Prince Charming has been delayed but he'll arrive one day."

Eric pursued his train of thought. "You run your own business. Are you married?"

"No."

"So you're a career woman." Did she detect a note of censure?

"For the time being." Starr looked directly into Eric's eyes. "Do you have something against independent women who are successful in their own businesses?"

Eric shrugged his shoulders. "It's okay for women to keep busy until they get married. After that, they should stay home and be full-time homemakers."

Starr was speechless. It had been years since she had heard a man express such rank chauvinism. "You actually believe it's impossible for a woman to combine a career with marriage and children?" At Eric's nod, she was ready to shout, "This is the twenty-first century Eric. Get out of your sterile, unrealistic lab and join the human race!" Instead she stared at him. "With your attitude I now understand why you're not married. No modern woman would have you."

Her outburst had no effect on Eric's mien. "Oh, I don't know. I'm not married because I've never given the subject any serious effort or time. I'm sure there are any number of women who would gladly marry me under my stipulations."

Eric's arrogant words were unbelievable to Starr. For once in her life she was tempted to inflict bodily harm on a man! How wrong she had been about him. Her disappointment lay like a rock on her spirits. The man of her dreams hadn't materialized in one Eric Hammond.

She threw back her shoulders and tossed her head. "Perhaps I'll see you later."

Eric reached out, putting a detaining hand on her arm. "Hold up. You'll suffer with me at the Palace Diner," he ordered. "If I can't eat in the hotel, neither will you. See you there at six o'clock."

"No, you won't. I have other plans," Starr was quick to retort. She wasn't surprised he had issued her an order—not an invitation. It was all in keeping with what he had revealed about himself. She wanted a man to be considerate and thoughtful, not arrogant and authoritative. The nerve of the man.

Then Eric cut away the ground under her refusal. He said quietly, "Please, change them."

With those blue eyes almost humbly begging her, Starr capitulated, "At six, Eric. I'll see you at the diner."

Against her will, thoughts of Eric kept intruding in her consciousness. He was a contradiction. A chauvinistic, arrogant male one minute, then the next a vulnerable person could be glimpsed under that shell. At least, she hoped it was a shell. Perhaps she could make the real man come to the fore.

It was well she didn't have to design a new travel brochure. It would have test tubes all over it! Also it was a good thing she didn't believe in magic or she would have been disappointed. Though a so-called love potion had fallen on him, Eric had shown no sudden lovesick attraction to her. Instead, he had shown a side of himself that wasn't appealing.

Still, the idea of a love potion tugged at her interest.

People had been falling in love throughout the ages without assistance. People weren't puppets on a string. She wouldn't accept such a fate for herself. When a man fell in love with her, it would be because he saw lovable things in her, not because his will was controlled by a powder.

At five o'clock, Starr closed her small office, which rubbed elbows with the Percy Drug Store on one side and Clinton's Hardware Store on the other. She walked at a leisurely pace down the quiet tree-lined streets. The well-kept houses nestled in green lawns, with gardens full of pink impatiens, white and purple petunias, and red geraniums. To her right, between tall pines, she glimpsed the green-blue waters of Oteango Lake. The scent of pine and lilac filled the air. Soon it would be time for the Lilac Festival she always enjoyed.

Arriving at the New Age Store, she took one last look about her. This was her town; she loved every inch of it. As she loved her business, which filled her daily with a sense of accomplishment and pleasure.

When she opened the door of the store, the bells at the top played an eerie tune. The black star-studded chiffon drapes that concealed the entrance to the back workroom parted. Glenda swept into the room, her long saffron gown billowing about her.

"Oh, it's you." Hiding a smile behind her hand, she said, "I was hoping it was one of my paying customers. Business has been slow today."

"Thanks. I did buy that darn crystal bottle from you at an outrageous price, or don't you remember?"

When Glenda nodded, a large hooped earring fell. Starr stooped and picked it up. "Here's your earring." She smiled at her friend's attire.

Glenda's black headband had a large zircon diamond at the center, surrounded by smaller stones of rubies and emeralds. Her cherub face and cupid doll lips made her look an unlikely candidate for the role of white witch she sometimes claimed to be. Starr appreciated the shrewd Irish business head under the flamboyant headgear.

"I've called the other stores, but no one has heard of Astral Industries. I guess she'll show up in her own time."

"Oh, well, I think shampooing is getting the glitter out, thank goodness." Starr gave a deep sigh. She actually liked to see the glow about him; it made him special in her eyes! "To complicate our relationship, we've lost his briefcase with his research in it."

"You do get into the worst predicaments. I can't look into a crystal ball and find the briefcase for you, but I can update your horoscope—"

"Not on your life. You've made enough trouble for me."

Starr didn't like the look creeping into Glenda's eyes.

"This horoscope would be a good one for you. Besides, you have a mystical name. It wasn't a coincidence you were named Starr."

"Naturally. Mother was into astrology, remember? Don't get swept away with all this mumbo-jumbo. I know it's good for business, but you and I know better."

"This time it's different. The stars determined who would buy that crystal bottle. It was meant to be you."

Starr threw up her hands. "Stop, stop, stop. I don't want to hear more. Give me a practical suggestion to get rid of the glitter immediately."

"Shave his head."

Picturing Eric bald made Starr burst into laughter. Glenda joined her.

"For sure, he'd murder me if I suggested it," Starr said when she'd calmed down. She jumped up. "Time for me to meet Eric at the diner. I forgot to tell you he can't eat in the hotel dining room because he won't take off his hat."

"What hat?"

Starr's explanation had Glenda shaking her head in disbelief. "Brother. No wonder he's irritated with you."

The Palace Diner was no palace. It had been years since Starr had eaten there. She shuddered as her nose was assaulted with the smell of onions, frying meat, and old grease.

Eric was in the corner of a back booth, his elbows on the table, head in his hands. He was staring at the scarred tabletop. He looked so tired she had an immediate desire to take him in her arms. She wanted to smooth away the tired lines with feather-light kisses.

She took herself in hand. Not too many hours

ago she was ready to slug him for his insufferable arrogance!

After greeting him, she slid into the opposite bench seat. His smile lit up his face and creased the star lines at the corners of his eyes. A warm flutter of delight hit her stomach.

"You're a beautiful sight for my tired eyes to behold."

His words so startled her she dropped the menu that the waitress had handed to her.

"Thank you. I'm glad you think so," she managed to say, knowing her face had become pink.

"Go ahead and order. I've already done so." His grin at the waitress had her smiling back. His effect on women appeared to be universal was Starr's thought.

"I'll have a hamburger with a salad on the side. Italian dressing. And a large soda."

"Good thing you didn't order the chili," Eric said after the waitress left.

"That good, huh?" She grinned at him.

He smiled back. "I thought the food was hot in Mexico City, but I was wrong."

"I've never been there. Did you like Mexico?"

"I attended a medical conference. I actually didn't go out of the hotel the three days I was there."

"How sad to be right there and never see the

magnificent ruins." She had a sudden glimpse of the lonely, dry-as-dust existence Eric lived. She ached for him. He needed someone to open the doors of his sterile, medical world to the delights of what was outside. Perhaps this would happen during Eric's stay in Rural Springs. She could dream, couldn't she?

"Can you tell me what you're working on at the lab?"

Eric plunged right in. His technical explanation soon had Starr floundering, but she loved the sound of his voice. She managed to make the right sounds, pretending she understood it all. Tomorrow, she vowed, she would get on the Internet or go to the library and learn what it was all about.

Becoming aware of the dazed look in Starr's eyes, Eric gave a chuckle. He apologized, "Sorry, I got carried away."

"No, no, I really did learn a lot."

Eric gave her a knowing grin. "Thanks for being so kind. Are you through eating?"

"Yes, indeed. You shouldn't eat here any more."

"What do you suggest?"

"Room service until we solve your hair problem."

"Only if you join me. I desire company with my meals."

Starr hesitated. "Let me think about it. But I'll ask Aunt Maud to give you a special menu."

They left the diner.

A gentle breeze stirred the leaves until they filled the air with a haunting melody. The sky was a deep blue and studded with diamond lights.

"It's such a beautiful night for walking," Starr said after she stepped out the door. Impulsively, she reached out and took Eric's hand. Hers felt small and fragile clasped in his big one. She looked up at him and smiled. His returning grin made her feel closer to him.

They talked about books on the way back. He liked biographies and murder mysteries. She liked reading romances for relaxation. Though he had given a low chuckle, he didn't deride her for her preference in books.

When they reached the Inn, he steered her toward the patio and one of the benches. The spicy fragrance of the lilacs filled the air.

Looking up, Starr saw speculation darken his eyes.

"I've waited patiently for you to tell me what's going on. Now you're going to tell me the real story about this powder and glitter."

Chapter Three

Starr gasped at the surprise attack. Of course, Eric was too intelligent to accept, without probing questions, her evasions about the powder in the bottle.

"Well . . . well . . . the contents of the bottle were supposed to have special effects—nothing to do with the glitter, however."

Eric's left eyebrow rose. "Go on."

"If a pinch of the powder is thrown on a man, he will fall in love with the woman throwing it."

"What absolute rubbish!"

"I didn't believe in it," Starr hastened to say.

"Or you wanted to make sure it would happen by pouring the whole bottle on me!"

"Now don't be ridiculous!" Starr's face turned a deep pink. "I hadn't even met you. It was a pure accident the contents fell on you. Besides," she ended triumphantly, "you didn't fall in love with me."

"Most definitely."

Eric's answer made Starr's heart feel as though it had been twisted painfully. Up until this moment, she hadn't realized she had been hoping he would fall in love with her. She hid her feelings and continued to explain. "Even though I didn't believe in a love potion, I thought the bottle would make a great conversation piece. By accident, the powder landed on you. You walked under the balcony at the wrong time."

Eric stood up. He began to pace back and forth. Starr's attention centered on his hair. The glitter, though much dimmer now, made him the fantasy Prince Charming come into her life for real. . . .

Another train of thought intruded.

What if there were some truth to the theory of reincarnation? Eric and she might have met in lifetime after lifetime and fallen in love with each rebirth. They could have met on Mount Olympus, made love in the olive groves, and worshipped at the shrine of Apollo at Delphi. He had become her knight in shining armor, battling a fire-eating dragon and taking her to his castle. He had suffered with Washington at Valley Forge and danced with her at a Continental Ball. They might have traveled by covered wagon to the valleys of Idaho . . . and now they were in Rural Springs.

"Earth to Starr. You haven't heard a word I've said."

Starr felt the flush spreading over her cheeks. "I'm sorry. What were you asking?"

"Explain how this love potion works."

"How should I know? The directions don't give us that information. You just believe it's so."

Her flippant answer brought a scowl to Eric's face. His full, sensuous lips pursed into a straight line, and his words came as no surprise. "Except for reading about witchcraft and supernatural events in the King Arthur legends, I've never thought anyone, in this day of scientific knowledge, would buy—actually spend good money— for a magic potion."

"Didn't you hear me? I bought an exquisite bottle filled with a sparkling white powder. I didn't buy it as any magic dust."

Eric walked around the room, his black eyebrows still drawn into a frown. He stopped in front of Starr. "Love potions—magic. Why am I wasting a single thought on such trivial hogwash?"

"I'm certainly not asking you to do so," Starr

cried. "But you asked about the powder, and I've told you all I know."

Eric scowled at her for a timeless moment. Then he threw back his head and laughed. "Forgive me. I'm acting like a fool when you've honestly tried to explain it all to me."

Starr nodded her head and accepted his apology with a small smile.

"Did Glenda buy only one of these bottles?"

"She bought six. She still has the other five."

"Why didn't you tell me? You know I wanted to test—"

"You wanted to test what was in my bottle. Besides, the others aren't the same."

"How different?"

"No glitter. Only white powder."

A wide grin spread across Eric's face, gentling the hard lines. Starr felt a stirring of hope. Were heart-stirring smiles a hint of a warm person inside?

He looked at his watch. "Too bad it's so late. I'd appreciate it if you'd ask your Glenda to see me after dinner tomorrow. I'd like to examine the other bottles."

Starr shrugged her shoulders. The scientist was back. "If you insist. I think you'll be wasting your time."

Eric didn't argue the point. "Actually, I could

use a chance to test something outside of my field. Perhaps my investigations at Glenda's will do the trick." He teased, "Of course, if you had followed directions and thrown a pinch . . ."

Starr threw him a disgusted look. She walked toward the side door of the Inn. "I'll see you tomorrow."

Later, Eric whistled as he headed for the shower. "You are the one," he sang while shampooing the last of the glitter from his hair.

A love potion had been in Starr's bottle.

Or so he was supposed to believe. No magic dust was necessary to get his hormones humming when he came close to the enchanting Starr. Quite a reversal to his usual response to the opposite sex. In fact, ever since he registered at an inn catering to honeymooners, many things were changing in his life. Was contact with happy newlyweds changing his beliefs about love? The thought was no stranger than believing a love potion actually worked!

He dragged his thoughts to the immediate problem. Why was Starr's bottle the only one with glitter? To be checked on later to validate the claim that it did contain the magic elixir?

Yet he understood it had been a random sale. He had had it dumped on him by accident.

Starr's bottle.

Though he didn't believe in love potions, he had had an immediate reaction to her. From the moment he looked up into her captivating green eyes, his world tilted, and it hadn't righted itself yet. His common sense had also seemed to desert him.

He hadn't, however, known she was holding back information, regardless if it was information hard to put credence in.

To give her credit, Starr said she didn't believe in the potion. She also had called him foolish for wasting a minute on plans to test the other five bottles. Was this her way to tell him she wasn't interested in falling in love at all—magic potion notwithstanding? Why did this bother him? Since he would be leaving soon, he wasn't interested in getting into a relationship.

He felt Starr would never consent to a brief affair. He imagined she was a woman who desired an engagement ring on her finger, a trip up the altar, and vows to love forever. It wasn't hard for him to picture the house she would want—many bedrooms and baths for the children and a big yard surrounded by a white fence.

Yet she seemed dedicated to her business, a career woman. Which picture was the right one?

Her kind of life wasn't for him. To live in one

place, day after day, year after year. The thought
had him shuddering. He'd feel trapped in a prison.
No grass grew under his feet. He needed the stim-
ulation of new challenges in new places. Still, he
had to confess he was enjoying his tenure in Rural
Springs, different as it was from any place he had
stayed in. It had to be the people—especially one
female! He looked forward to tomorrow.

The next evening Eric was impatient to get to
the New Age Store.

His long stride and fast pace made it difficult
for Starr to keep at his side. Lost to him were the
glories of the masses of flowers in the gardens,
the fragrance of the lilac bushes, and the diamond-
studded night sky.

With a yank he opened the door to the New
Age Store. His gaze fell on Glenda, and his mouth
fell open.

Glenda's multilayered gown of chiffon swirled
with the colors of the rainbow. A black cape fell
from her shoulders to the floor, held together by
an enormous pin in the shape of the moon and
sun. On her head a heavy turban of gold cloth was
slipping down her forehead. She raised her hand
to push it back in place.

Starr rushed past Eric, laughing.

"Glenda, you idiot, take off that heavy turban

before you fall flat on your face. Why are you dressed like this?"

With a grateful sigh Glenda removed the turban. "I have a wealthy, eccentric customer coming tomorrow who expects me to dress like a high priestess of magic. I was trying on the outfit. Do you think I'll impress her?"

"You impressed me," Eric said. "Wear the turban but take out some of the stuffing. How about a wand as well?"

Glenda looked him up and down. Her eyes lingered on his black hair. "You must be Eric."

He bowed from the waist. He clasped her hand and planted a kiss on the back. "What title do you have?"

Glenda laughed good-naturedly. "You're a good sport."

The assorted objects around the store and in the display cases had Eric's attention. He wandered down the aisle, and his finger lightly set in motion the crystals dangling from a gold rod. He peered closely at small, exquisite silver figurines of witches and sorcerers holding small crystal balls.

"Glenda, the workmanship on these is outstanding." He reached behind the front ones to pick up one of Merlin, teaching the young Arthur. "I'd like to buy this one. The daughter of a friend of mine would go wild over it."

He quickly scanned the packed wall shelves. Boxes of incense, packs of tarot cards, packages of magic tricks, wands, colored stones, and minerals vied for space. The crystal bottles he was interested in weren't there. His heart sank. Had Glenda sold them already or, worse yet, emptied them?

"Where are the five bottles with the infamous love potion?"

"Starr told you?" Glenda looked closely at him. "You're being very calm about it."

"On the surface, my fair lady. It isn't every day a mere mortal is the recipient of . . . er . . . magic dust."

"I'll get the bottles." Glenda disappeared behind the black curtain. She hurried back with a small box. The crystal bottles with their ornate stoppers were placed on the counter.

Eric carefully picked up one and held it up to the light. As Starr had said, the white powder had no glitter in it. He turned it in several directions.

"Starr, did you notice if your bottle had small etchings of fairies around it? You can see it only if you hold it a certain way."

Starr picked up a bottle and examined it.

"You're right."

Eric laughed. "When they made these to sell, Astral Industries didn't miss a trick. Fairies are magical creatures. They wanted you to believe their sales pitch."

"Why do you think they put glitter in only one bottle?" Glenda asked.

"Someone became cost-conscious and figured it was cheaper to leave it out of the product," Eric mused.

He turned to Glenda. "Do you have any objections if I take these bottles to test them and see if they contain any unusual ingredients?"

"None." Glenda added, "I'd like to know what's in them."

"Me, too," Starr agreed. "The quicker the better."

At the lab, the results were in.

Common, harmless talcum powder filled the five bottles.

"Very wise choice by Astral. Throw that on someone and no harm done—and no law suits," Eric muttered to himself the next day.

He doodled five-pointed stars on his blue blotter. Not the powder but the other ingredient in Starr's bottle had played havoc on him. Was the glitter the magic substance?

On the surface, it was an easy conclusion. But, was Starr's the real thing and the others duds? Or was it the other way around? Since she had washed it, he couldn't test the contents of Starr's bottle. How did he test the others for an unknown love ingredient?

Since Starr had taken hers out of the running, the answer had to be in the five remaining bottles.

Eric picked up the phone and punched in the number. He waited for Starr to come to the phone, his hands busy rearranging some test tubes. "Starr, please be at Glenda's at eight tonight. I've a back-log of work so I'll be late getting home from work."

"Wait, Eric. What were the results?"

"Tonight. I haven't time right now. Good-bye."

Too late, Eric berated himself for being so abrupt with Starr. She didn't deserve such treatment. It wouldn't have killed him to talk to her about the results.

At eight o'clock, Eric placed the five bottles in a row on top of the showcase.

"Talcum powder," he said with no fanfare.

"That's it?" Glenda shrugged her shoulders. "Why doesn't it surprise me? But I have to admire a great sales promotion by Astral Industries."

"The idea of a magical powder making two people fall in love has its appeal. . . ." Starr's voice trailed off.

"If that's true, that will be my line when I try

to sell the remaining bottles." Glenda reached for them. "They'll make a unique gift for Christmas."

"Don't touch those bottles," Eric ordered. "I'm not through with my investigation."

"What in the world are you planning?" Starr protested. "You've already tested the powder."

"My test only confirmed the powder is harmless and has no detectable foreign substance in it." Eric grinned. "Can magic be put in a test tube? Apparently not."

"So?"

"We can test the contents in another way."

"All right. Tell us."

Eric had a smug look on his face. "We'll throw a pinch from each bottle as directed on selected persons."

"No!" came the strangled protest from Starr.

Glenda's eyes, on the other hand, lit up with the prospect. "Let's do it."

"Since I haven't fallen in love with you, Starr, your bottle didn't have any magic." Observing Starr closely, he was interested to see disappointment in Starr's eyes in the split second before she lowered her gaze.

He continued, his face bland. "Since these five bottles have the same powder, it could be in all of them." Tongue-in-cheek, he added, "Although Astral implied all the bottles contained a love potion, we know that Starr's must have been a placebo. Why Astral did this, we don't know. Maybe we'll get the answer in the future. In the meantime, we'll do our own testing."

Eric noted Starr's continued frown of disapproval.

"Yes. I'm all for it," Glenda agreed.

"No, no, no," Starr repeated. "I don't believe in magic, but I'm superstitious about some things. It's bad luck to tamper with matters best left alone."

Starr's continued resistance appealed to Eric's streak of perverseness. He wanted to tease her, to make her eyes flash and her cheeks turn pink with emotion. When he threw out the suggestion to test the potion on people, he hadn't been serious. Now, the idea grabbed him.

"We should prove or disprove the theory that there is a love potion which works on human beings. This'll be a welcome change from the serious testing on cancer I do all day." Eric laughed and turned to Glenda. "They're your property. What do you say?"

"By all means, do it." Glenda fairly trembled with excitement.

Starr shook her head, but the two ignored her. She asked, "How are we going to do it, Eric?"

"Since we have five bottles, we'll pick five couples. The person throwing the pinch will be given just enough information to encourage him or her to participate. Then we'll wait for the results. If there aren't any, we'll know it was only an intriguing sales gimmick."

"How long do we wait?" Starr asked. Her voice was laced with sarcasm. "A minute, a day, a week, a mo—"

"Okay, you've brought up a good point," Eric agreed. "Shall we wait a week and see if there's a distinct change in the feelings between the man and woman? Maybe, we'll be lucky, and it'll be love at first sight. We'll label Starr's bottle as Number One."

"With whom shall we start?" Glenda wanted to know. Then she laughed. "Take me as the first test rat!"

Starr stared at her. "Just who do you want to fall in love with you? You've always declared you didn't want a man cluttering up your life and living off your money."

"Mayor Steven Fields."

Chapter Four

"Y ou're not even on good terms with him, Glenda," Starr cried. "A battle royal has been going on for months because he won't give you the building permit to expand your store."

"You're right." Glenda grinned with glee. "But won't I enjoy having him grovel at my feet. The permit will be a token of his undying love."

"You'll do this to get your permit?"

"Yes."

"Please, don't. It's all wrong." Starr turned on Eric, trying to ignore his attractive smile, which spread to light up his eyes and erased the harsh lines around his mouth. "You'll be meddling in people's lives, not an inanimate object in a test tube." Starr took a deep breath. "If the potion works, will Steven have his heart broken—"

"I'm sorry, Starr," Glenda apologized. "I didn't think you'd react like this. Don't worry about Steven. I often think he doesn't have a heart, only a calculating, shrewd mind. That's why he's a good candidate for this test. His pride might get wounded, but that's all. And I'll have my permit."

Somehow, Glenda's offhand remarks didn't ring true to Starr. Was there something going on between Glenda and her old classmate Steven other than the permit? Did she have a hidden agenda about her offer to be the first test person?

"I'll get some drinks," Glenda said, and vanished into her back room.

While she was gone, Starr looked everywhere but at Eric. His casual approach to the testing irritated and disappointed her. He should be treating it seriously or not at all. People, real people, were going to be involved. Their deepest emotions and desires could be stirred up. This wasn't a trivial prank.

Glenda returned and said, "Let's get the show on the road, fellow conspirators."

Eric picked up Bottle 2. With the names Glenda Donavan and Steven Fields on the label, he gave it to Glenda. "Here. Record the time and place. Hopefully, we'll have results right away." Eric grinned in Starr's direction. "Like love at first sight, as promised by Astral."

"Do we have to do this human testing?" Starr asked again. "What will happen when Steven finds out we've made a guinea pig of him? He'll never forgive you, Glenda."

"I'm going to do it." Glenda rotated her shoulders to relax them. "I need the addition to my store." She gestured at her crowded shelves. "Room for more merchandise, conference rooms for classes in psychic healing, seances, and psychometry—and much more. You've no idea how many people are asking for stuff like this. I love it! For this, I'll enter Daniel's—no, Steven's—den of lions."

Glenda called Starr at lunchtime the next day. "I got in touch with Steven, and he's coming to the store tonight. I don't know the exact time because he's got a dinner date with his feather-brained secretary, Brenda Henderson."

Well, well. Could Glenda be jealous? Starr wondered if she would be if Eric told her he was taking out his lab assistant. Since he wasn't hers, he was free to go out with any willowy redhead or gorgeous blond he chose.

However, since pouring the love potion over his impressive head, she admitted having an unreasonably possessive feeling about him. Though the glitter had washed out now, she still, for a brief moment, saw a glow about him. It made a shiver run down her spine. It made him so special. . . .

The potion.

To her annoyance and grief, it was the mixture that claimed his attention while he ignored her and her opinions. Fortunately, it also made him forget temporarily his briefcase, which still hadn't been found.

Her attention returned to Glenda. "Why is Steven coming to your store? I thought he insisted business transactions be discussed only in his office at City Hall."

"I fibbed a little. I said I twisted my ankle and would appreciate it if he'd come to the store this once. You know I can't very well throw the love potion on him in City Hall with all those people milling around."

Glenda confessed, "To him my store is pretty far out. He's become so sober and critical. When we were kids, we used to have a good time together. He even took me to the junior prom."

"I remember. Your red satin chemise with the fringes made you look like a Roaring Twenties flapper. Steven couldn't keep his eyes off you." Nostalgia filled Starr. "We had such fun back in those days."

"Too bad we have to get older." A gusty sigh issued from Glenda. "Anyway, Steven's coming to see my revised plans. I'll bet he's hoping I cut my addition in half."

"You're still determined to do this? I wish you wouldn't," Starr urged. "I hate to think what he'll do if he ever finds out. In high school he'd have laughed about it, but you know he's changed since his wife died and he came back to Rural Springs."

"I've got to risk it. I'll call you after Steven leaves tonight. Bring Eric with you."

In the background was a murmur of voices.

"A client just came in," Starr explained. "Have to hang up now. See you later."

Eric.

Just thinking his name made Starr's heart trip over itself. Had the magic dust been thrown on her, these out-of-control feelings might make some sense. She was playing with fire. She shouldn't risk having her heart broken this time— really broken, not just cracked, as had been the case before.

The emotional high she experienced whenever Eric came near her was unnerving, especially since he treated her in an impersonal and disinterested manner. Sometimes she felt he barely hid his irritation with her. She even thought he was doing the testing in order to annoy her. So, why was she still drawn to a man who wasn't interested in marriage and scoffed at love?

Was it because she couldn't resist the challenge he had tossed at her? Her desire to change the lifestyle of an entrenched bachelor? To want to make a difference in a lonely, barren life? Probably, all of these reasons!

In the late afternoon, dark clouds rolled in from the west. At six o'clock a drizzle fell. By seven, it became a steady rain.

After Glenda called, Starr found a big black umbrella. Eric and she huddled together under it as they walked to the store. When they both stepped into a deep puddle, a chuckle rumbled out of Eric.

"I haven't walked in the rain like this since grade school," he said.

Starr gave a giggle. "I love it. Since I'm not made of sugar, this rain won't melt me." She ducked from under the umbrella to let the rain pelt her uncovered head.

Eric pulled her back under the umbrella. He looked down into her smiling face. His hand gently pushed back the wet hair from her face.

"I think you're kinda sweet," he whispered. "So maybe you are made of sugar. I need to taste—"

For a breathless moment Starr waited for him

to kiss her. He didn't disappoint her this time. His lips pressed hers and contentment filled her.

"Ah," he said, "sweeter than honey."

Starr opened her eyes and gave a soft sigh. What was she to do now? She looked away from Eric in confusion. He never did more than kiss her once! Thankfully, she saw the swinging store sign and said, "Here we are."

She dashed into the door, leaving Eric to close the umbrella. She hoped he put it to drain against the side of the building.

"So, what happened?" Starr asked.

When Glenda turned around, she mirrored the gloomy weather outside. Her shoulders drooped and no smile curved her lips.

"Oh, no. I'm not sure I want to hear this."

"It could have been worse—I think," was the answer. "You did warn me, Starr."

Eric lounged against a showcase and kept silent. Starr urged Glenda to sit down. "Why don't I make us some strong tea?"

"I need it." Glenda heaved a deep soulful sigh.

"Ah, come on. You've got to be exaggerating," Eric finally spoke.

"You're right," Glenda laughed ruefully. "It didn't go the way I'd planned. There wasn't any burst of sizzling chemistry or immediate declaration of love. Far from it." She shook her head in disbelief. "However, we did agree to give the potion a week's trial. Time will tell."

Glenda held up her ankle for their inspection. A strip of dark blue, star-studded material was wrapped around it.

"I couldn't find an ace bandage so I used this. A good choice, wasn't it? I even remembered to limp around. When Steven looked at my ankle, his eyebrows went up. I was lucky he gave my injury the benefit of the doubt. He sure doesn't take me and my business seriously."

Starr looked at the astrology signs trimming the black tablecloth, then at the blueprints rolled out on top of the table, held down in one corner by a crystal ball on a gold pedestal.

"When you decorate the table like this, can you blame him?"

"I know," Glenda agreed. "I overdid it this time, but I needed the props. Was I ever nervous." She looked slyly at Starr. "Besides, I wanted to be sure to follow the directions. That one pinch had to be right."

"Get on with your story," Eric prodded, his fingers tapping the top of the showcase.

"When he bent over the blueprint, I threw the pinch dead center on the top of his shiny blond head. It disappeared in his hair." She took a deep breath. "I was so relieved to do it. Then Steven literally bellowed. I almost dropped the bottle."

"What made Steven so mad?" Eric asked.

"He had just seen the new room I added to the blueprint. He reminded me that he thought the addition was too large already, and I was crazy to expect him to okay an even larger one. He said this was the last straw."

Glenda flung her hands wide. "Then he lowered the boom. He wasn't ever going to give me a building permit because this larger addition obstructed the view to Oteango Lake."

"Oh, Glenda," Starr said softly, "I'm so sorry. What did you say?"

"I begged him to reconsider and repeated all my old arguments for my permit. I even promised to make the addition smaller." She paused for breath. "He ignored me. He made me so mad and upset that, before I could stop myself, I burst into tears."

"Very unwise," Eric said with a quick shake of his head. "When women cry to get their way, men hate it. You should have controlled your emotions and stayed calm."

Starr threw him a murderous look. How could he be so hard on Glenda? Did he always have to be so cold and unfeeling? The last thing Glenda needed was to be bawled out by another man.

"Don't pay any attention to Eric. He's just standing up for his species, right or wrong."

Starr gave Eric another glare before putting her arm around Glenda's shoulder. She gave her a hug. "Drink your tea. When you feel up to it, tell us the rest."

Glenda looked grateful for the sympathy.

"He told me to stop crying my crocodile tears. His mind wasn't going to be changed, not tonight or any time in the future. With that, he left, slamming the door so hard the bells at the top fell off."

Glenda took a swallow of her tea, the cup shaking in her hand. "The evening wasn't supposed to end this way. He should have been declaring his undying love, not his undying refusal to give me my building permit! So much for magic power to make a man fall in love." She sat up straighter and plastered on a bright smile. "Don't worry about me. It's not the end of the world."

Starr looked closely at Glenda. She was putting on a good front. Steven and Glenda had been an item in high school. Starr herself had thought they would marry some day. What happened to prevent that, Glenda had never told her. Now Steven was back in Rural Springs and he was a widower. Had her friend been hoping for the potion to work—and not just for the permit?

Starr watched Eric go to Glenda. He began talking quietly to her. Glenda laughed at something he said.

So Eric could be compassionate and kind. A warm rush of feeling filled Starr. Starr looked back again in time to see Eric place a kiss on Glenda's cheek.

He walked to Starr's side and held out his hand to her. When he smiled at her, his gaze was warm and tender. Starr's heart felt strange and fluttery.

"Let's leave," he urged. "It's getting late and I've persuaded Glenda to go to bed and not give up on Steven just yet."

The rain had stopped. The moon played hide-and-seek with the dark clouds. They walked slowly on the dark village street, skirting the puddles on the sidewalk. Starr was content to leave her hand engulfed in Eric's large, comforting one. She returned the squeeze he gave hers.

Starr broke the silence. "Do you like living in a small village?"

"It takes some getting used to. I'm basically a big-city dweller. I've lived in apartments and hotels. I haven't a clue about the difference between a weed and a flower." He gave a chuckle. "The thought of taking care of a lawn is chilling." He looked down into Starr's wide eyes. "I've enjoyed the peace and quiet of Rural Springs. It's been a change."

"Do you like moving around from city to city?"

"Yes. I get restless if I stay too long in one place. Besides, the nature of my work forces me to travel. That suits me."

"Don't you miss having a family or roots or friends?"

Eric shrugged his shoulders. "Not so far. I don't think of those things as being important. I have my research and it's all that matters."

"Oh. . . ." Starr couldn't ask any more questions.

Eric's answers had shot down her hopes for a meaningful relationship for them. Eric's stay here was temporary. He was a solitary man by choice and content to stay that way. He needed only his all-consuming work. He would leave her behind without a thought.

She needed roots and family. She wanted a man who would hunger for her and be content to come home every day to his fireside—no tumbleweed for her. She couldn't imagine herself staying in a hotel waiting for him to come home from a lab somewhere.

Furthermore, the thought of giving up her business made a shudder course through her. She had worked so hard for too many years to throw it all away just because a man had antiquated ideas about the role of wife and mother. Besides, she had to work, to keep busy and active.

At the back of her mind, she had envisioned having a family, but keeping an office at home, to combine career and family easily.

Had Eric's mother stayed at home and thus became his ideal model for a wife? If this was his background, it would be difficult for him to change. For the two of them to find happiness together, each would have to change and compromise. Was this possible? Could love, deep and all-encompassing, transform them into a husband-and-wife team?

Even though the differences between them seemed insurmountable, she still nursed the hope that love could make all things possible. He did have some positive thoughts about his stay here. It wasn't much but perhaps enough to have the sprout grow to a mighty oak.

The next morning Starr's thoughts were filled with the wonder of the kiss they had shared. It had lasted a fraction of a minute but its effect would last forever in her heart.

At least for her this was true. She had to remember that Eric was a wanderer. Perhaps a kiss was just a kiss, and nothing more to him.

Pulling her thoughts back to mundane matters,

Starr concentrated on locating the briefcase. She tried to suppress her superstitious fear that finding it would hasten Eric's departure. Last night's conversation kept upsetting her and destroying her belief that things could get better.

Another search of the premises was fruitless. No employee, full or part-time, had any connections with pharmaceutical companies, as Eric had questioned.

Starr called Eric at his lab and reported the depressing news.

"Contact everyone who checked out of the Inn the day I arrived," he suggested. "The briefcase may have left with them."

"Good idea. I'll get right on it."

It was a perfect summer night. The pale yellow moon hung near the horizon, bathing the world in a mystical light. A playful breeze conducted a concert with the leaves. A riot of flowery fragrance permeated the shadows.

Inside the New Age Store, the delights of nature were replaced with a mantle of gloom.

They made it official.

Bottle 2 had no love potion in it.

A week had passed and Steven hadn't sought out Glenda. He hadn't come to her with a heart-shaped box of chocolates or a big bouquet of traditional red roses—not even a thorn. He hadn't sent her any love poetry. Instead, he had rudely taken her parking spot in front of the grocery store!

"Let's not get discouraged. So two bottles were duds, Starr's and yours. We still have four more to go. That's not a bad sample." Eric sat, his long legs stretched in front of him, in the back room of Glenda's store.

Starr was delighted that Steven hadn't fallen in love because of the potion. She was sorry for Glenda, since she had a nagging feeling her friend might be harboring deeper feelings for Steven.

Starr accepted Eric's word that the love potion hadn't affected him. She kept counseling herself not to hope he would soon fall in love on his own—with her. Longing for a normal relationship, free from the contamination of magic, cascaded through her like a torrent.

"I hope you're going to stop this testing," Starr said. "Even magic can't overcome all obstacles. You and I were complete strangers, and Glenda's motive for using it was too mercenary. She wanted to get her permit as a gift of love, without love on her part. Love has to be shared. How do you control this experiment to ensure that criterion?"

"We'll continue to test," Eric stated emphatically. "Since I may have missed something, I want to examine the bottles again. The difference from Starr's bottle is obvious—the glitter in my hair proved it. Perhaps the fairy etchings have a hidden clue."

Close examination of the bottles showed the exquisite drawings to be identical.

"My tests found no foreign substance in the bottles. That doesn't rule out a subtle something I failed to detect. We have to continue testing it on people as the label directs."

Watching Starr's expressive face, he said blandly, "Just because neither Steven nor I fell in love isn't conclusive. We may even be using the wrong timetable."

Seeing how determined Eric was to continue, Starr decided to help to get it over with as soon as possible. She surprised Eric by saying, "I'll pick the next couple for the test, one way or another."

Chapter Five

Starr stared at her young secretary, Melanie
Hopkins.

Melanie needed a husband.

When Harry died two years ago, he left her with
a small daughter to raise. Unable, or not wanting
to cope alone, she lived with her parents, who had
catered to her. Last month, though, her father retired, and her parents moved to Florida. For the
first time, Melanie had to stand on her own two
feet, and she had trouble doing so.

Melanie turned on her computer to find the
screen didn't light up. She pressed the ON key
again—nothing. She flipped through the manual,

biting her lower lip in concentration, then hit the suggested keys. Nothing.

"Starr, I've broken the computer! I can't seem to do anything right."

Starr was ready to agree with her. Melanie should stay at home being a wife and mother, while a strong and capable husband worked and handled every aspect of her helpless life.

"Calm down. I'll call the repairman."

Chandler Endicott promised to be there in an hour.

Starr put Melanie to work straightening the supply closet. Melanie hummed a song as she worked.

Waiting for Chandler, Starr doodled Fourth of July sparklers on her blotter. Eric, her Prince Charming, dark and splendid in all his early luminous glory, was never far from her thoughts. She began to regret her reckless promise to find a couple.

She and Eric hadn't chosen each other. The magic hadn't worked as it was supposed to do. Glenda had chosen Steven with no results. Today the onerous job of making the choice for someone else was hers alone.

Melanie's humming made her sit up straight. Melanie? No, too shy. She wouldn't do anything on her own to attract a man. She'd die of shame before she would throw a pinch of love potion on a man. That would be too forward. A lady never took the initiative.

So, she'd have to shamelessly trick her into doing it. But to whom? Chandler was on his way over. He'd be a challenge for the experiment. He was a widower and had stated his determination to stay one forever. Besides, his mother made his life comfortable. If one could believe half the stories, his marriage hadn't been a happy one. He might be just the right husband for Melanie. He had that aggressive man-in-charge aura. As she had done with her late husband, Melanie could sit at his feet and adore him. She'd fuss over him as his mother was doing.

Starr, in all honesty, jeered at herself. She had her weak moments when she dreamed of doing the same with Eric. Adore him, make plans with him, and fuss over him. Make sure he ate properly and got enough rest. Since pressure at the lab was increasing, he looked harassed and tired. She longed to hold him close to her and smooth away all his cares with her kisses and caresses.

These thoughts helped her to let the negativity she had had about the testing slip away. She'd be doing Melanie and Chandler a service by giving them a chance to find each other.

Calling Melanie into her office, she held up the crystal bottle.

"That's beautiful," Melanie exclaimed.

"It's more than that."

Starr silently prayed to the heavens for forgiveness for the whopper of a story she had suddenly thought of to tell Melanie.

"It's filled with a special headache remedy. Chandler suffers from severe migraines, but he refuses to try it. His mother appealed to me."

Melanie's eyes were so trusting that Starr almost stopped. The thought of pleasing Eric and getting this testing over with made her hurry on. She swallowed the guilty lump in her throat. "Chandler would suspect me, but he'd never expect you . . ."

"I don't understand what you want me to do."

"When Chandler is working on your computer, I want you to throw a pinch of the headache powder on the top of his head as his mother asked me to do."

"Starr," Melanie objected, "you're not making sense. How can a pinch of powder on someone's head help—"

"I know. I don't understand it either, but I'm following his mother's directions." Starr crossed her fingers behind her back and took a deep breath. "I think she's a customer of the New Age

Store and Glenda has some pretty far-out things to sell." Starr looked away from Melanie's guile-less eyes.

"If you're sure you want me to do this . . ." Me-lanie's voice reflected her uncertainty. "Only don't ask me to talk to Chandler. I'll do it when his back is turned. He's so big, and I don't know him very well."

Chandler breezed in an hour later. Melanie opened the door for him. Starr saw his startled reaction to the blush dyeing Melanie's flawless cheeks and the sweep of her long lashes as she quickly lowered her gaze to look at her feet. For a moment, Starr was sure, time stood still for Chandler.

"My computer is over there," Melanie managed to say, still not looking at him. "It won't come on."

Giving his head a shake, Chandler sat down be-fore it. Starr watched him compose himself. Good. Melanie, with her shy beauty, had caught Chan-dler's attention.

Melanie faded back behind him. Starr quietly walked up to her. She handed her the open crystal bottle and silently mouthed, "Throw a pinch on Chandler, now."

When Melanie raised it above Chandler's head, her hand shook. She cast an imploring look at

Starr. Starr nodded her head up and down vigorously and gave Melanie a hard stare.

Melanie screwed her eyes shut and threw the pinch of love potion, just as he turned his head slightly. Her throw was wide. It landed on his nose.

"What the ... ?" Chandler swore under his breath at the distraction. He brushed the powder away and kept on working.

Melanie gasped and ran into Starr's office, thrusting the bottle safely into her outstretched hand. With a sigh of resignation, Starr brewed a cup of tea for Melanie to calm her before returning to Chandler.

He rose and began to put away his tools.

"That was fast. What was the trouble?" Starr asked.

"Someone dropped the back of an earring into the keyboard."

Starr groaned. Melanie, with her tendency to drop things. She prayed, please, please, let there be a love potion in Bottle 3!

"You're looking happy this morning," Starr commented to Melanie the next day. "Did you have a date last night?"

"My daughter, Amanda, and I went to the Presbyterian Church Social."

"So? What happened?"

"Chandler Endicott came and sat with us. He was very sweet with Amanda."

"Chandler entertained Amanda? I didn't think he liked children. His first marriage was childless. From choice, I understand."

Melanie blushed. "You know how appealing Amanda can be. For a four-year-old, she knows how to wind any man around her little finger. She was on a roll last night."

Starr's imagination took wing, and she saw Eric, smiling indulgently, being led by the hand of a giggling golden-haired toddler. A sturdy little boy, the image of his father, with black hair and deep blue eyes, followed her. With effort she listened to Melanie.

"She even asked Chandler if he was going to be her daddy."

"Chandler must have hit the roof."

Melanie blushed again. "Not at all. He told her we had to discuss it before he could give her an answer."

Starr's mouth dropped open. For heaven's sake, Bottle 3 had the love potion in it! Here was shy, retiring Melanie mooning around. Chandler—the last man on earth to consider marriage again— saying he wanted to discuss it. And all this happening in the space of a few hours, never mind the week they had agreed on. Melanie's next words jolted her.

"When I asked Chandler how his headaches were, he said he didn't have any. You told me he had them, didn't you?"

"I didn't. His mother did." Behind her back, both of Starr's hands had fingers crossed.

Melanie shook her head. "When I told his mother I threw the powder on his nose instead of on his head, she didn't know what I was talking about."

Starr groaned. Trust Melanie to blab everything. "What else did you say?"

"Since Chandler came up to me, I didn't think I should tell her everything you said. You know, about her going to the New Age Store for the remedy."

"Thank heavens for that! Listen, Melanie, promise me you won't say anything again to either one of them about this headache business. They don't want people to know."

"Fine with me." Melanie went to her computer. "I'm glad it's fixed. Chandler's so clever and sweet. You should have seen him last night. And Amanda just adored him." Melanie's hands rested motionless on her keyboard. She looked off into space, her work forgotten.

Starr sighed. She'd never get any work out of Melanie today.

Tonight, when she reported to them, Glenda and Eric would be insufferable. Bottle 3 could be the one to have the fatal magic. All this experimenting with a love potion didn't give Eric any ideas.

If there was magic in Bottle 3, why hadn't she been fortunate enough to buy it? No. Now she was getting so mixed up. Did she or didn't she want to believe? No, once and for all, she didn't. Love didn't come in a bottle.

Melanie had asked her how a headache could be healed by a remedy thrown on the top of the head. A headache couldn't. Neither could love be turned on by a tiny pinch of magic dust on one's nose.

It had become a habit for Starr and Eric to walk slowly each evening to the New Age Store, enjoying the fragrant breezes blowing across the tranquil lake and the beauty of the gardens along the flagstone walkway. Every time, Starr gave thanks to the universe to be able to live in such a serene village.

Tonight Eric held Starr's hand, swinging it back and forth as children do. They talked like old friends about their day.

Starr felt very close to Eric. She studied his profile from beneath her half-lowered lids. Fatigue lines bracketed his mouth. She wanted to reach up to touch those lines and erase them with her fingertips. As though he had read her thoughts, Eric looked down at her and smiled. Starr's breath caught in her throat, and her heart skipped a beat or two. He squeezed her hand and looked away. Starr repressed her disappointment. She had wanted him to draw her close and kiss her.

After they entered the store and went into the back room, Starr announced, "Bottle 3 may have had the love potion in it. I chose my secretary Melanie Hopkins and Chandler Endicott for the experiment."

"Brother," Glenda exclaimed. "You picked an unlikely pair. What about Amanda? I've heard Chandler dislikes being around children."

"Not any more."

Starr gave an account of what happened.

"It was love at first sight for the little charmer, and maybe for her mother, too."

"Whoa," Eric demanded. "Who are these people?"

Starr gave him brief biographies of her candidates and how she got Melanie to throw the powder on Chandler. When she got to the part where the powder landed, Eric and Glenda burst out laughing. Starr joined them—even when Eric, between hoots of laughter, mumbled, "Melanie, following in Starr's footsteps and being off the mark—"

Starr ignored him. "No matter where the potion landed, it evidently worked. From Melanie's glowing report of last night, I hope to hear wedding bells soon. Chandler strikes me as a man of action. Besides, Melanie needs to be taken care of immediately. I, for one, will be relieved when I don't have to solve her problems."

"Who would ever think this would happen?" Glenda walked to a chair and plopped down.

Eric recorded the happy results on an index card. He turned to Glenda. "Lock this bottle away."

"Definitely," Starr agreed. "We want to test each bottle only once." She shook her head slowly. "The more I think about it, it's only a coincidence and not magic at all. Chance brought Chandler to repair the computer. I chose him out of desperation. It was Melanie's shy beauty which captured his interest and his heart. There was no magic here at all. No way."

Eric shrugged his shoulders and turned to Glenda. "Can you remember the exact words the saleswoman used? Did she say all the bottles had the love potion? Was the whole bottle filled with endless pinches of love magic or only one pinch? Did she—"

"Stop, Eric. Honestly, I can't remember. I think she said all of them had it, but she was such a vague, fluttery woman I didn't press her for details. I didn't even notice that the bottle Starr bought was the only one with glitter. You were the living example of that fact, Eric."

"I sure wish Starr had bought a plain bottle. And it was my bad luck she didn't follow the directions. A pinch of glitter powder wouldn't have made me into a blinking ornament."

Starr gave a moan of protest. "You know it was an accident. I never wanted to throw anything on you. But right now, I wish the bottle had fallen on you!"

Eric looked at Starr. When she defended her actions, she looked adorable. Her green eyes were like shining emeralds flashing daggers at him. The delicate skin on her cheeks turned pink, and her voice rose in pitch. He wondered if she was controlling an urge to stamp her foot.

"Who'll be next?" Glenda asked.

"I don't want to have anything more to do with it. You and Glenda can have all the honors." Starr turned away from them and looked out the window.

"You can't duck out on us, Starr Evans. You

started it all," Glenda protested. "Even though I've already done my part, I'm willing to think about another couple."

"It's your turn, Eric," Starr declared. It was time for him to take some responsibility for his project.

"I know so few people in this village," Eric protested. He smiled and said in a beguiling tone, "But I have an idea you'll save the day, Starr. You were never at a loss when it came to my hair."

Unable to think of an appropriate defense, Starr turned her back on him. Suddenly she wanted to get away from Eric and—drat the man—his charm. She mumbled a good-night to Glenda. Quickly she ducked out the store before the others realized her intent and could stop her.

"Wait for me," Eric called.

When he caught up to her, she ignored him. He remained silent until they reached the dark shade of the tall lilac bushes. He laid a hand on her arm and stopped her. Without warning, he put his arms around her, pulled her close and kissed her. The spicy scent of the lilacs wafted to their lips, adding to the sweet taste of his kiss.

The kiss—ah, it was sweet as honey, thrilling as a high-speed chase, and breathtaking as the down-sweep of a roller coaster.

Starr took a deep breath and opened her eyes. She gazed up at Eric.

"Couldn't you see I was only teasing you?" he asked.

"I shouldn't be so sensitive."

"I've never known a woman like you," Eric said softly. "I hope we'll always be good friends."

Friends? That's all he wanted to be? Desolation swamped Starr.

"Of course," she answered, pasting a bright smile on her face. Never would she let him suspect she had been thinking of more than friendship for them, that the kiss had left her wanting more.

Maud was waiting for her niece the next morning.

"I've never had such a strange guest as Eric Hammond. Thank goodness he isn't wearing those outrageous outfits anymore. Why did he come here without a bride on his arm? Why—"

"Whoa, Aunt Maud. Give me a chance to answer your questions."

"Why did Eric register here?"

"Because we're rated the best hotel within fifty miles." Starr gave a chuckle. "Besides, he didn't read our brochure."

Maud straightened the registration book on the counter. "Come into my office. Tell me what you know about him."

Maud enjoyed Starr's humorous account of

Eric's hair predictament. After a moment's hesitation, Starr also told her about the love potion and the decision to test it.

"Three left, you say?"

"Yes, and I again foolishly promised to find another couple. I shouldn't help Eric so much."

"So, that's how the wind blows!" Maud's eyebrows rose. "I suspected as much. You've been with him every night."

"You're reading too much into this. We're just friends."

Maud suddenly hugged her niece, a big smile on her face. A trill of laughter pealed out.

"Let me pick the next couple! I know the perfect pair. They'll test the notion of a love potion. Never, in a million years would these two fall in love under normal circumstances. I'm not even sure it'll work with supernatural power."

"Who?"

"Millicent Dean, my housekeeper, and Allister Kingsley, my chef."

"No, Aunt Maud, not those two!"

Chapter Six

"Millicent has had a ridiculous crush on boorish and opinionated Allister for years. What a dear, sweet woman like Millicent can see in him, I'll never know. But if she wants him, I'll help her. Your love potion may be her last resort."

"No, we shouldn't tamper with an older person's life. Do you want Millicent to be tied to a man like Allister forever? They're in their fifties, aren't they? You know how hard it is to change at that age. From what I've seen, Allister is set in his ways."

"Don't get upset. On the one hand, you say it isn't a love potion. Then on the other, you act as though it were true. So far, there's no evidence of it for Eric or Steven, and you believe Melanie and Chandler's attachment was a natural outcome. That's a one hundred percent failure score. So, it won't work for Millicent. No harm done."

"Aunt Maud! Of course there'll be harm. I assume you want her to know about the love potion—not a wild story about a headache remedy as I did with Melanie. You know she'll be filled with hope and be broken-hearted if Allister doesn't fall in love with her."

Maud had the grace to look sheepish. "You may be right, but Millicent should be given a chance to win the man of her heart."

"All right, have it your way. I'll get Bottle Four. Ask Millicent to talk to me tonight. I'll be frank and urge her to think seriously before she agrees to do this."

Starr stood up. "About Eric's briefcase. Where can the darn thing be?"

"We can only wait and hope someone will come forward with it. That's all we can do." Maud patted her niece's arm. "Try to convince Eric we haven't forgotten about his briefcase."

After dinner, Starr and Millicent had a glass of sherry in Maud's sitting room. Through the open windows a soft breeze billowed the sheer lace curtains. The night birds chirped their evening song.

The sky was fast darkening to the deep blue of night. The evening star burned brightly on the horizon.

"Forgive me for getting personal, but do you think Allister is the man for you?"

Tears filled Millicent's eyes, and a sigh seemed to issue from the bottom of her soles.

"I'll always love him. If only he would realize it, he needs me so much. The poor man has no one to love him or to take care of him. I'd devote my life to him."

"Please listen carefully to what I have to say." Starr took a deep breath. "Don't be in a hurry to make a decision."

Just as Starr feared, Millicent was thrilled with the story. "Yes, yes, I'll do it. Oh, Starr, finally I'll have my darling Allister."

Starr handed her the bottle.

"It's beautiful," Millicent gushed, examining the fairy etchings and the crystal beauty of the bottle. "Just what one would expect to contain a love potion." She read the directions. "I only need to throw a pinch on him? Do I throw it on his head when he's looking at me?"

"Heavens, no. Don't let him know. Do it when his back is to you."

"This is so thrilling. Like being in the movies!"

Starr watched her leave the room, clutching the

bottle to her breast. She was fifty-two years old, almost as round as she was tall, with blue eyes and graying hair. She was no beautiful heroine out of a romance book, but it didn't matter. When cupid's arrow of love pierced a lonely human heart, age and physical appearance mattered not one whit.

And what of Millicent's Romeo? Starr gave a rueful laugh. A thin six-foot-tall man with stooped shoulders, a hooked nose, and hollow cheeks. His hair made a thin gray fringe above his large ears. Most people found him unattractive, both physically and in temperament. But Millicent loved him.

Self-loathing swept over Starr. Who was she to be judgmental? Millicent and Allister were entitled to fall in love, even if they needed a boost. Maybe the love potion, if it was real, was transitory in nature and was there only to provide a spark. After the initial explosion, love would have to be nurtured and fed by day-to-day actions and commitment.

There hadn't been any sparks or anything else with Eric or Steven. So why was she worrying?

The next evening Starr and her aunt drank their tea in silence.

Millicent had poured out her story of tribulation and verbal abuse at the hands of Allister.

"You said you had a love potion and I believed you! How could you do such a terrible thing to me? To raise my hopes! I followed the directions perfectly. The powder landed on top of his head." She gave moan. "Then he turned and roared as if I had thrown a firebrand on him. Since then he has complained about everything. And the hateful looks he throws at me are like daggers to my heart. Oh, I wish I had never been born. I don't know if I even want to work here anymore."

She burst into tears and left the room before they could console her.

Remorse filled Starr.

"I'm sorry, Aunt Maud. If only I hadn't told you about the love potion. Now you may lose your best housekeeper."

"Don't be silly. You had no way of knowing this was going to happen. You did warn Millicent, but she willingly used it. Believe me, matters between her and Allister aren't any worse than usual. Her heart was set on the impossible happening. Since she'll never go away from Allister, she'll continue working for me."

"What does she see in him? He's so obnoxious. It's a good thing his ill humor doesn't affect his delicious meals."

"We can't all have the same tastes, Starr. Here's your test bottle. It's a dud, like the others."

Starr looked at Bottle 4. She felt satisfied with the failure. Tall, gangly Allister Kingsley with his vinegar personality and sweet, plump Millicent were an unlikely couple. Yet, who was she to judge? She didn't know what went on in Allister's mind and life. He must have some redeeming qualities Millicent saw and admired enough to want to live with him for the rest of her life. She herself saw Eric as having great possibilities as a lover and husband which others might not.

Starr, however, felt regret and sorrow for Millicent's loss. Maybe a stronger dose was needed in some difficult cases. More than a pinch, but not the whole bottle.

Starr threw up her hands.

Heavens, she'd fallen back into the trap of thinking the potion was the genuine article. Of course it hadn't worked for Millicent, nor would it work for anyone.

On Friday, Starr arrived at the New Age Store before Eric. Bored, she wandered around the store.

"Glenda, I don't see any new merchandise. Have you stopped buying?"

"For all intents and purposes, yes." Sparks of anger filled her gaze. "I haven't any room. If I knew I could start building my addition, I'd find the room. I'm so disgusted with Steven. Since the night I threw the love potion on him, he won't listen to reason or even talk to me. When you warned me not to tamper with fate, you were right."

"I wonder why Steven is so opposed to this addition. It's well planned, and it'll bring in more business to the village. Surely, as mayor, he wants to see Rural Springs grow. Do the two of you have a feud from your high school days?"

"No. Soon after the prom he began to date Margie, and later married her. I lost contact with him after that."

"Has he made attempts to renew old times?"

"He was happy to see me until I told him what I was doing. He didn't mince words to tell me I was wasting my talents. He thought I should have gone into law. That was in the yearbook, you know. But law has never been exciting enough for me. This store is what makes me happy." Glenda raised her shoulders in a shrug. "Steven has to accept me as I am."

"I think there's more."

"Yes. He thinks I'm going to spend too much money on this addition. He's not paying for it, so it's none of his business how I'm going to finance it."

"Maybe he's concerned about your welfare."

"Yeah, sure. So he makes life difficult for me? He's just impossible. Enough about me. What's been happening with Millicent and Allister?"

Briefly, Starr filled her in on what had happened. "We'll have to scratch that bottle. Only two more to go, thank goodness."

"Is Eric coming tonight?"

"He expected to, but he's been working long hours. The research isn't going as well as they had hoped without the notes in his briefcase."

"You still haven't found it?"

"No, but we've not given up yet."

While Glenda busied herself rearranging the figurines on the shelf, Starr examined the American Indian dream catchers. Ah, if only she could capture her dreams and make them come true.

Her finger set one swaying from side to side. Her gaze and her thoughts followed the gentle motion of the feathered circle. It was like her relationship with Eric, drifting back and forth. The glitter problem and the decision to test the other bottles had them working together. Now, overtime at the laboratory had kept him away. She didn't fault his dedication; she admired it. But she did miss him.

Starr turned away from the window. "About all we've learned so far is the love potion may have worked on Chandler. Honestly, Glenda, I never expected a cold fish like him to be so romantic. He sent roses to Melanie this morning, and he's taking her out to dinner at the Inn. Talk about moonlight and roses. It's all there in their relationship."

"What about Amanda?"

"That's another miracle. He does everything she asks of him. He even bought her several outfits for her Barbie to keep her busy tonight while he wines and dines her mother."

The phone rang.

"Hi, Eric, are you coming tonight?" Glenda asked. "Do you want to talk to Starr?"

She handed the phone to Starr.

Starr took a deep breath to still the rapid beating of her heart. It was always like this. It didn't matter how many times she heard Eric's voice.

"We're sorry—"

"How about you?" he asked in a low voice.

"Yes, of course." She quickly went on to tell him about Millicent and Allister.

"I'm not surprised," he said. "We can write off that bottle." After a pause, he said, "I'll see you tomorrow. Good night, my Starr."

The last was said so softly that Starr didn't know if he really said "my" Starr. She could only hope so.

"Well, we don't have to wait any longer for Eric," Glenda said. "Since I ran a sale today, I was busy all day. My feet ache. I'm in need of a good, long soak in the tub with a mountain of bubbles," Glenda said. She drew down the shade on the front door and hung the CLOSED sign. "Let's go home."

While Starr and Glenda visited together at the store, Eric worked at the lab. He got up from the lab stool and stretched. Another dead end in his work. Discouragement and frustration plagued him tonight.

After he looked at the clock, he knew it was too late to see Starr at Glenda's. He called and got the news about Millicent and Allister.

The bright spot in his life was this potion business. Of course, there was no scientific reason to pursue the issue. But it kept him amused and looking forward to a new development—especially what Starr would do next! Also what he would do. He found himself speculating about the emotion called love . . . which was supposed to have occurred when the potion spilled over his head. Love hadn't, but the accident sure made him think about it seriously for the first time in his life.

The tale of the potion had been a successful sales pitch to an impressionable storekeeper. He wondered how many bottles were being sold around the country. Perhaps it could be their next avenue of research.

Astral Industries.

Even the name was in keeping with the merchandise packaging. To add to the mystery, where was Astral located? It wasn't listed with the Better Business Bureau or anywhere else. Would they find out when the trial period was over and the salesperson reappeared to check on the results, as promised?

Glenda's description of the pleasingly plump, fluttery woman with a black cape and a straw hat didn't fit his idea of a salesperson.

Originally, he had been asked to consult for four weeks on the chemotherapy project. Now, Dr. Thorpe wanted him to stay on longer. Since Eric had decided to take him up on the offer, he should find an apartment and move out of that honeymoon inn. But did he want to tie himself to a lease, be stuck in one place?

On second thought, he'd continue to live at the Inn. He could pick up and leave on short notice.

His thoughts returned to the testing.

Was there or wasn't there magic? How could they prove it or disprove it? Just saying there wasn't any didn't do the trick. What was the proof going to be? Was it possible to even get a definitive answer? As a scientist, he honestly didn't think it was possible to prove or disprove something in the realm of fantasy. This was the stuff of dreams, or just believing. And rightly so. To reduce love to a textbook formula would destroy it forever.

So far, the pinch thrown on Chandler may have been the real thing. From all reports, Chandler was behaving like a man smitten with the love bug. Should Chandler and Melanie be urged to marry as soon as possible just in case there was a time limit to the potency of the love potion? Eric had no idea how long the magic was supposed to last. Such a test he hadn't even considered conducting. The wisest move for Chandler would be to get married as soon as possible.

Millicent and Allister had been the supreme test for any love potion. He chuckled. It was no wonder it had failed.

Glenda's motives were something else. Anti-love? Maybe not. Eric wasn't too sure about Glenda. When she had been making those statements about Steven, she hadn't looked him in the eye. After all, she and Steven had known each other for years. What was underneath all their sparring and fighting? Resisting the attraction that pulled them together?

Two more bottles. Then it would be over.

Who would be willing to do the testing this time? Eric mulled over the issue. So far, the persons concerned had been well known to Starr and Glenda. Was there anyone in this lab he could approach—all in the name of science?

At first, Eric rejected the name that popped into his head. Many reasons why he shouldn't ask him came to mind. Still, why not? What's the worst he could do? Refuse? Laugh?

Chapter Seven

Ping . . . ping . . . ping . . . The small stones hit the sliding glass door of Starr's bedroom.

Almost asleep with a book in her hand, she bolted upright at the sound. Sliding out of bed and belting her robe around her, she sped across the floor to the railing of the balcony. It was a dark night with clouds blotting out the light of the moon. She leaned over and ducked a thrown stone. Eric looked up at her. A big smile wreathed his face.

"Eric! What are you up to? Why didn't you just call me on the phone?" she whispered, not wishing to disturb the sleeping guests.

"Where's your sense of romance?" Lowering

his head to his chest in mock dejection, he said, "You've wounded me to the quick."

"Don't be silly." Her smile was full of delight. "I'm flattered. It's like being fourteen and having my own Romeo."

"Much as I adore gazing at the most beautiful woman in the world, I'm getting a crick in my neck. Come down to me. I have to talk to you—among other things." He twirled an imaginary handlebar mustache and leered at her.

Starr's soft laughter floated down to him. "Give me a few minutes." Her head reappeared. "I'd much rather you climbed up to me."

"Hah, my fair maiden. You know there are no strong vines or a sturdy tree for me to climb."

"Excuses, excuses," mocked Starr, and disappeared.

The Inn was dark and quiet at two in the morning. The Twilight Bar had closed an hour ago. The patio was empty. The ground lights along the garden paths cast a golden glow. Starr ran barefoot over the flagstones of the patio to where Eric waited for her. She stopped short.

"Well, why did you come tonight?" She sat down on a stone bench and tucked her bare feet under her. Eric took a seat beside her.

"Sorry I didn't get to Glenda's as planned. I

couldn't wait until tomorrow to tell you my choice for the next test."

"Is that the only reason, Romeo?"

"Of course not. When I saw the light, I had to see you." He took her hand and placed a kiss on the back of it. "I'm always glad to be with you. What happened to my hair gave us many opportunities to be together."

"Your shiny hair made you very distinctive."

"Yeah. I'd rather be a plain joe."

"Tell me about our new victim. I hope you're going to be very honest with him or her."

"I'll ask my supervisor, John Thorpe."

"Your boss? Is that a good idea?"

"He needs the distraction of our different line of research."

"Okay, but don't say I didn't warn you." She stood up and started walking slowly to the door. She didn't want to leave him, but she had to deny the dictates of her heart and be practical. "Much as I hate to say it, it's very late and we both have to get up early. We should go to bed."

"A good idea." Eric took her arm and they started to climb the stairs.

At her opened door, Starr turned to say good night. Before the words were uttered, Eric leaned down and placed his lips on hers. The touch created a surge of delight which coursed through her with a zing. For a moment her lips clung to his before she pulled away.

"I–I think I'll say good night."

"Okay," Eric whispered. He let her go.

Starr leaned against the closed door and murmured, "Be still, my heart!"

A most interesting evening.

Dr. Thorpe welcomed Eric's interruption at nine o'clock. He pushed aside the computer sheets on his desk.

"What can I do for you?" he asked Eric.

"Are you submitting another request for a federal grant for our research? Any chances?"

"Not really. Have to go through the motions for the last time. Any suggestions?"

Putting his hands in his lab coat pockets, Eric wandered around the room. Dr. Thorpe leaned back in his chair and waited.

"A new line of research has opened up for me," Eric finally said.

"Good. I need some encouragement."

"This has nothing to do with our cancer project, but it may bring the money you need—in a backhanded way."

"Why are you so nervous?"

"It shows that much?"

"Yeah. So tell me."

"Okay. You haven't been able to persuade Angela Moreland to give a donation." Thorpe nodded. "My suggestion is far out," Eric continued.

"How far out?"

"Would you be willing to use a love potion to make Angela fall in love with you?" Eric took a deep breath and plunged on, "Women in love are known to grant anything to the object of their desire."

Dr. Thorpe threw back his head and laughed, the sound filling the room.

"Good grief, man, a love potion? What witch cast a spell on you?"

"Actually, a golden-haired beauty with green eyes and a dimple in her cheek."

His meeting with Starr and the testing they had done was quickly told. "Since we have two bottles left, why don't you try Bottle Five on Angela?"

John Thorpe was silent, the look on his face quite grim. "My feelings for Angela are apart from my professional need for her money. I don't want to jeopardize my future personal relations with her."

"Hopefully she has feelings for you, too. So far, you haven't gotten to first base with her. This could speed things up. Would it be so bad to be in love with each other?"

"I don't know. I feel a little ridiculous. A love potion?"

"I felt like you. One possibility does exist in the case of Chandler and Melanie. The chance of it being in Bottle Five is infinitesimal but, what the heck. Take a shot. Treat it like one of our experiments. You had no idea how they were going to turn out, but that didn't stop you."

"Okay, but don't tell anyone in the lab about this line of research. A love potion." John shook his head. "It will take a long time before I dare tell Angela. Don't women use this method? A man should be more direct. I don't know . . ."

"Do it when you feel comfortable about it, John. If you decide not to, it'll be fine with me."

Eric left quickly. He sympathized with his supervisor. It was an absurd and ludicrous proposal to a logical, scientific man. Yet, it grabbed one's fancy and wouldn't let go, as he well knew.

He thanked the heavens Glenda had been gullible enough to make her purchase and that Starr had bought one of the bottles. How changed his life had become because he stepped under her balcony at the right moment.

For the first time in his life, he had found a place to sink roots into. He had been encouraged to see the lighter side of life, to laugh with Starr, to do the silly testing with Glenda. How much easier it was for him to be touched by Starr, and to touch and kiss her in return.

Much as he hated to admit it, he was beginning to believe, not in magic, but in fate. There was no way to escape his destiny—and his Starr. Eric laughed at the pun, but he knew it was true.

With difficulty, he turned his attention back to his research for the remainder of the day.

John Thorpe's phone call interrupted Eric's preparation for bed.

"Even though your story boggled my mind, I've decided to take a chance. We need more money for our research. I'm willing to accept any donation, regardless of the limitations attached to it by Angela." He chuckled. "How can such an appealing, beautiful woman have so much steel under all her silk and perfume?"

"I don't think we men will ever understand the so-called weaker sex."

"Not when they make up their minds! I've already called Angela so we can again discuss her possible donation to the Center—on her terms. She'll come to my office tomorrow at eleven."

The next morning Eric placed the crystal bottle on John Thorpe's desk. But with Glenda's warnings still ringing in his head, Eric reached to take the bottle back. He didn't want to be responsible for an unhappy ending. Before he could put it back into his pocket, John entered his office.

"Is that it? It looks harmless enough."

Eric handed it to him with reluctance. "I warn you again, there may be some unwanted results."

"Warning received. I'm willing to take the chance." His smile was broad. "What dire ending can there be? Angela doesn't fall in love, and we'll be back to square one."

"Remember what happened to Glenda. Angela may not only withdraw her support permanently, but may drop you out of her life completely."

John shrugged his shoulders. "What will be will be. Frankly, I'd like this chance to win the woman of my heart."

Eric gave up. It was remarkable how just talking about the stuff exerted its power to make people act against all rational thought. No one in his right mind, and definitely not research scientists, should play with the supernatural.

John Thorpe—he had expected him to reject it with a hearty laugh.

Eric groaned silently as a chill inched its way up his spine in warning. "Don't use the potion. I—"

"What? You've told me it didn't work for you or Glenda or Millicent. Why are you stirred up about a harmless white powder?"

"I didn't tell you the whole story."

"Ah, now it comes out."

"I think the powder is harmless in very small amounts. In larger doses—"

John laughed. "You told me to throw only a pinch. Are you now suggesting I throw the whole bottle on her in order for it to work?"

"NO! Don't ever do that." Eric paced in front of the desk. "When I came here the first day, I wore a baseball hat."

"Yeah, I remember."

"The reason for it was what happens when you have the whole bottle dumped on you. My hair was covered with powder and glitter."

Dr. Thorpe was speechless for a moment. Then he chuckled. "No wonder you covered your head. I suspected something was wrong with your hair, but never this. What happened?"

Eric related the story of the accident and his difficulty washing out the glitter.

John looked closely at the bottle in his hand. "I don't see any glitter."

"Right. Only Starr's bottle had it. Why, we can only guess. The other five bottles have plain talcum powder. However, since we've tested only a pinch from some of the bottles, we don't want to take a chance using more than the pinch. And we can't say your bottle is the same as the others. It may be that even a pinch this time is too much."

John was adamant. "Angela's hair is blond. Even if a pinch makes it glisten, it won't be a tragedy." John went on, "I can't see why your past problem should keep me from using the potion. This bottle has no glitter. I'm going to assume the plain powder will have no harmful effect."

"No physical harm, John. Relationship harm— maybe. Don't forget, I've warned you."

John shook his head and walked Eric to the door.

"Angela will be here in a few minutes. Check with me later in the day."

Eric hadn't heard from John by the time he left the lab that evening. He called Starr.

"Want to walk down to the store? I need some fresh air. We can tell Glenda what little we know."

"Love to. I'll meet you in the lobby."

Starr's heart gave a skip of joy. She hadn't expected to be with Eric tonight. He was becoming an obsession with her. Without him, time dragged and the day was cloudy.

When they started their walk, he took her hand in his. A ripple of desire flitted up and down her nerve endings. A touch of his hand—how could it produce such a powerful effect? She looked up at Eric. He seemed oblivious to the effect he had on her.

"It's beautiful tonight." Eric pointed to the sky. "Did you see that shooting star?"

"Yes, and I wished on it. Did you?"

"I didn't know I was supposed to. If I do it now, will it count?" he teased. A week ago he would have scoffed at anyone wishing on lights in the sky. What was happening to him?

"It will be fine, I think." If only his wish would be the same as Starr's. When Eric took her hand in his, she dared to dream of their future together.

"You've been rushed lately with your brochure business, haven't you?" Eric asked.

"This time of year is always hectic for me. We've picked up ten new clients. Of course, every brochure needed to be done the day before yesterday. How are things at the lab?"

"Even though John had some doubts, he decided to be part of our experiment."

"How much did you tell him?"

"Everything—even about the glitter in my hair."

"Oh, no."

"It was okay. He had a big laugh over it. He was glad to know the reason for my attire when I first came to the lab. Since he didn't call me at the end of the day, I don't know how his conference with Angela came off."

They walked along in companionable silence.

Eric broke it. "It's good to be together again."

Starr stopped walking and looked at Eric. Dared she read more into his words? She lifted her face toward him. Her lips parted and she held her breath, waiting for his kiss. His head began to descend. She slowly closed her eyes with a contented sigh and leaned toward him.

His lips, warm and soft, met hers.

"I could get addicted to this," said Eric, and he kissed her again.

When Starr heard the giggle of a teenager passing by, she broke the embrace.

"We . . . we . . . should get to the store before Glenda closes," she said, feeling the blood rush to her cheeks.

Eric gave a low chuckle and agreed.

As they continued the short walk, Starr kept silent, letting her thoughts race on. Though her breath had left her, her head had whirled, and her blood pounded in her veins, she didn't have a clue as to how Eric was affected. He had been so quick to stop.

Could the differences between them be bridged by a slow but deepening friendship? A friendship that could even lead to affection, love, and passion? Not every love started with the blast of trumpets and the clashing of cymbals.

Eric wasn't a demonstrative man. In addition, he was a rolling stone. His work prevented him from making lasting friendships or relationships. Rural Springs was just another one of his temporary sojourns. How could she change his way of life? Even a love potion, which should have power, hadn't affected him. Still, Starr couldn't squash the little hope that whispered all wasn't lost yet. Not as long as he continued to kiss her and seek out her company almost every day.

A disturbing thought surfaced. She had been thinking Eric was the one who had to change. But what of herself? Would she be willing, for the sake of love, to transform her quiet existence, uproot herself, to follow Eric? Wasn't his work important for the good of many people? Didn't it outweigh her travel brochures? Yet she loved her business as much as Eric did his research projects. And she didn't want to move away from her beautiful mountain village.

Starr wanted to hold her head and groan. There were so many questions which defied a right or a wrong answer. She had been under the illusion that love would smooth out the rough edges and solve all problems easily.

She was wrong.

Of course, she had never met a man like Eric. All her male friends had come from a background that was similar to hers. They were comfortable like an old pair of shoes, too alike to sustain a lasting interest in each other, as time had proved.

It was a relief to reach the store.

"Glad you came," Glenda said. "I was about to go home. I had a big shipment come in today, and I've had a time trying to find room for it all. The shelves are much too crowded. Hope you have a cheerful report for me."

"Sorry, no news about John Thorpe," Eric replied. "Starr and I needed to get out and take a walk."

"A walk? That's all?"

"It's become a relaxing habit coming here." Eric answered. "Besides, Starr's company is soothing."

Soothing? That's all she was to him? As comfortable as old leather moccasins? So to him, the kisses weren't escalating with passion. Could it be his lips pressed hers only to toy with and tease her? No more! Not even if the possibility of one more kiss would push him over the edge into the sea of love.

Eric turned to Starr. "We should let Glenda finish up and go home."

On the walk back to the hotel, Eric was bewildered by Starr's cold rejection of his attempts to converse.

What did I say to upset her? Women. I'll never understand them.

Chapter Eight

The next day, Eric found John Thorpe standing by the large window in his office. His shoulders slumped and his chin drooped to his chest. Behind him, rain trickled slowly down the pane of glass. Dark storm clouds raced across the sky. In the distance came the low rumble of thunder.

John's body language didn't spell victory.

"Good morning. How did things go yesterday?"

John reached into the drawer and handed the bottle to Eric. "No problem throwing the pinch on the top of Angela's head during our discussion."

Eric waited.

"Angela left last night for an indefinite visit to Paris."

"What? Did you know about this?"

"I hadn't any idea she'd planned this trip. It's as though she ran away as quickly as she could. Some love potion you gave me!"

"Well, your motive—"

"It wasn't for the money. I threw the potion on her because my heart had other desires. I wanted her to fall in love with me. So, you can't accuse me of misusing the spell."

"Why do you think she left town?"

"She has no interest in me. End of story. Period." He shrugged his shoulders. "I won't blame this development on your potion. Even magic couldn't overcome the lack of romance on Angela's part."

Eric paced before John's desk. "I'm sorry. What amazes me is how we let this love potion get under our skin like a worm in an apple. Its power lies in our willingness—even eagerness— to deceive ourselves. To believe what one wants to believe, in order to escape reality."

"Well, there's no love potion in Bottle Five."

"Sometimes I have this irrational wish for the magic to work the impossible on Starr. That there was a world of love in the bottle she dumped on me. She's so lovely. She makes me think and feel as I've never felt before for a woman. Whether it's love, I wouldn't know, since I've never been in love before. Hard to believe at my age."

"You'll have no trouble knowing if you're in love," John said. "It'll turn you upside down and back up again, until all you want to do is be with her. My wife had that effect on me all the days of our marriage. I've been very lonely since her death. Angela has tilted my world for the second time. Love potion or no, I'm not giving up on her. Paris isn't the end of the world."

"Thanks, anyway, for helping us with our experiment."

That evening, on their way to the store, Starr and Eric walked into the deep shadows of the border lilac bushes. When he reached for her, it felt right to go into his arms. She threw her past resolve away. His lips, demanding and warm, covered hers. His arms held her in a tight embrace, as though he'd never let her go. Yet, he didn't kiss her again. And he let her slowly slip away from him, with a look in his eyes she couldn't interpret.

"Glenda's waiting for us." Starr's voice was firm and didn't betray her confusion at his actions. Why did he kiss her, only to draw away? And why was she foolishly letting him do it again? She should have her head examined, especially since his cool acceptance of her suggestion showed no emotional upheaval on his part.

"Yes, we need to get on," Eric said.

She was puzzled by the stern look on his un-smiling face. Her troubled thoughts made her glad to reach the store.

Inside, Glenda paced back and forth before them. "What happened to Dr. Thorpe and Angela Moreland? They've been on my mind all day."

"Angela left for an indefinite stay in Paris last night. She left—*poof*—no good-bye, no letter. Like she couldn't get away fast enough," Eric said.

"Told you to warn him."

"I did. He claims he threw the pinch so Angela would fall in love with him. No misuse of the potion by him."

"No love potion in Bottle Five." Starr voiced her satisfaction. "I think this testing is a waste of time. Let's stop now."

"Not so fast," Eric protested. "We still have one more bottle."

"Eric! Don't you ever give up?"

"I'm with Eric," Glenda broke in. "Why not test the last bottle? If there's no love match, I can sell the bottles with a clear conscience."

Starr stared at the two of them. Frowning, she

gave in. "All right. As long as you don't come up with any more reasons to test the powder."

"Okay," Glenda agreed. "Who will be our last couple? With four failures behind us, I haven't much enthusiasm left."

"I don't know anyone." Starr stared into space.

"Even though I picked the last one, I'll try to think of someone," Eric said, his voice a pitiful whisper.

"We're getting nowhere. Come on, Eric, let's go home and see what tomorrow brings."

Starr was working on the hotel accounts the next morning. Her aunt entered the office. "Mind if I interrupt you?"

"Of course not. I hardly see you anymore. What's on your mind?"

Starr watched her aunt sit on the edge of the chair in front of the desk, a sign that she was hesitant about bringing up the subject for her visit.

Starr felt warm feelings of affection welling up in her. Aunt Maud was her favorite relative. She was generous to a fault, easygoing and comforting. Since Starr's parents had retired to Florida three years ago, she happily made her home with her aunt, helping as much as possible with the running of the Inn.

"Starr." Her aunt took a deep breath. "Do you

know how long Eric Hammond plans to stay here?"

"No idea. I believe he's been asked to stay indefinitely at the lab."

"Oh, dear, I hope not. That means he'll continue as our guest."

Starr waited for her aunt to go on.

"It's awkward having a single male registered among all our happy honeymooners. Doesn't it make him uncomfortable? What keeps him here?" She broke off her questioning. "Is he interested in you?"

Starr could feel the blood rush to her face. "I–I really don't know. What with his hair and testing the love potion, we've been together a great deal."

"Is that all? No midnight kisses?"

"Aunt Maud!" She blushed again. "We've kissed a few times, but that's all."

"He appears to be very eligible."

"My dumping the whole bottle of the potion on him didn't make him fall in love with me. We get along very well, but he has his emotions under control. He's not comfortable showing affection, and he draws away after every touch or kiss." Starr shrugged her shoulders. "Right now, all his attention is on the testing and not on me."

"That's too bad. How much longer will the testing take?"

"We've one more bottle. I hope we find this last couple right away."

"Umm." Maud looked at her niece with narrowed eyes. "Will you consider me?"

Starr stared at her aunt. A pink flush covered her smooth cheeks, and her fingers fidgeted with her gold bracelet. Starr realized anew that her aunt was a very pretty woman. Although she was fifty, she looked ten years younger. Her figure was trim, though slightly plump. Her blue eyes sparkled with good health and life.

"Why, Aunt Maud, you sly fox! Who is the man? You never date."

Maud sat up straighter in the chair. "That's why I'm going to be irrational and silly and resort to your impossible love potion. It's probably the only way I'll be able to get Ted Gardner to romance me."

"Dr. Ted? You've been friends forever."

"Yes, and I'm tired of it. He needs to have a fire lit under him. If he doesn't respond this time, I'm going to join a singles club or enroll in a dating agency."

Starr got up from her chair and rounded the desk. She hugged her aunt and kissed her cheek. "Good for you. Go for it! I'll go to Glenda's right now."

Starr hummed happily as she backed her car out

and drove to Glenda's. She liked Dr. Ted Gardner. When his uncle retired, Ted had begun his general practice of family medicine in Rural Springs five years ago. He looked and acted like Jimmy Stewart, slow and easy—and sexy! Starr understood her aunt's frustrated feelings. Eric was like Ted. Nothing short of a volcanic eruption was going to make him act quickly on any decision. Eric didn't seem to realize how time was speeding by. Her aunt was right for taking the initiative about her feelings for Dr. Ted.

How she wished with all her heart the love potion was in the last bottle. If not, she'd write a complaining letter to Astral Industries about their misleading sales promotion.

An hour later the last of the bottles was in the care of Maud Evans.

"Good luck, Aunt Maud. I've a good feeling about this bottle. Even if I don't believe in the notion, I'd like to see Dr. Ted fall under love's spell, by whatever means you need to use. It would also be nice to have my faith in humanity restored—that a person, even one seeking a sale, would tell the truth about the product."

"I'm getting nervous about doing this. Just holding the bottle in my hand gives me a strange feeling."

Starr grinned. "Pooh. Get Dr. Ted in the right

position so you can carry out your deed. I'd suggest you do it sometime tonight, when the moon is shining. From the bar, the romantic love songs of the forties fill the background—"

"Good day, honey. I don't need you to orchestrate my evening. Thanks, just the same."

"I'll stay out of your way, but I'll be rooting for you."

Starr and Glenda were alone that evening. Eric was at the lab.

"Your aunt and Dr. Gardner. It's hard to believe." Glenda started to fill their cups. "Try this new tea. It's special."

"Oh, no," Starr cried. She snatched her cup away. "No more of your magic concoctions for me."

"Don't be so suspicious. It's a special blend of India and herbal teas. Quite nice, I think. Try a sip of mine."

Starr did. "Umm. I like it." They sipped their tea in companionable silence.

"I'm thinking of attending the next village board meeting and going over Steven's head." Glenda gave a noisy sigh. "All they can do is say no."

"By the way, Millicent is still our housekeeper,

even though Allister continues to glower at her and make her cry."

"What about Melanie and Chandler?"

"They're our only success—if you're a believer," Starr replied.

Glenda gave a big yawn. "Let's go home."

As she drove back, Starr's thoughts took wing.

The love potion. Magic dust. The powder of enchantment.

It held center interest in their lives. And yet, it wasn't real. The only real thing was its power to ensnare and hold captive their thoughts and imagination. It propelled them into actions that could hardly be called sensible. It monopolized their time, day after day, and night after night. Invisible chains bound them to this quest. They wouldn't be free until . . . Starr realized she had no answer. A shiver swept through her, and she shook her head. She was being silly to let her imagination run away with her.

With a laugh she recalled a chapter from *Anne of Green Gables*. Anne believed her own imaginary ghosts were so real that she was terrified to walk at night through the woods to her friend's house.

There was no magic at work in Rural Springs.

Starr's common sense told her so.

Chapter Nine

Impatient to learn what had happened, Starr returned to the Inn for lunch. The dining room was crowded. Her aunt had no time for her.

She picked up her coffee cup and carried it outside to the patio. Finding an empty table, she sank into the chair, grateful to be away from her office duties.

"Ah, there you are," her aunt said. She put her cup and saucer on the table.

"How did it go?"

"Don't get your hopes up yet. Ted acted the same as ever." Maud made an apology for him. "Of course, when he finally got there, he was tired. He'd had several emergencies, which made his office hours longer than usual. I wish he didn't have to work so hard."

"You work hard, too."

"That's true, but I can take it."

"Ho ho, and you think the male is the weaker sex?"

"In some ways. Remember I'm the product of my age. I was taught men need to be coddled and babied and showered with creature comforts more than women. My problem has been I'm so good at it. Ted sees me only in the role of a comfort giver. And last night I did it all over again." She slumped against the back of her chair. "I don't think your magic potion has the power to change my character or Ted's."

"When did you do it?"

"No problem there. Ted was eating his sandwiches. I walked behind him on the way to get the coffee pot and threw the pinch. It disappeared without a trace in those iron-gray waves." She stood up and reached for her cup. "Nothing happened. There were no fireworks. Ted just said, 'Thanks for the meal.' "

"Don't get discouraged. It's early times."

"Working overtime?"

Behind her, Eric's deep voice penetrated Starr's

concentration. She dropped her pencil. It rolled to the floor. This was Eric's first visit to her office.

"I–I didn't expect to see you here. I thought we were going to meet at Glenda's." Her heart felt as though it had tripped over itself at the unexpected joy of seeing him. Without encouragement, a rising spiral of warmth and sweetness swirled through her body.

"Since the last pinch has landed on Ted's head, we've gone as far as we can." Eric wandered to the window and set the hanging ornament there swinging from side to side. "I like these things."

"It's an American Indian dream catcher."

"Really. You'll have to explain it to me someday." Eric looked around the office. "Is Melanie working for you?"

"Until she gets married. They're planning an August wedding."

"Do you still think they fell in love without the help of the potion?" His eyes were intent as he looked into hers. Her breath became shallow and difficult again. Drat the man!

"I haven't changed my opinion about that silly story of love magic," Starr answered.

Without warning, Eric leaned over and kissed her, taking his time. His lips were infinitely skillful and knowing. The almost unbearably sweet kiss made Starr feel she was flying, whirling around and around like a feather caught in a wind draft.

"I tend to agree with you," he murmured against her lips. "I like to be in charge of my life—as now."

The second kiss made her sigh with pleasure. Reluctantly, she realized she had to put a stop to Eric's casual kisses. There had been no words of love or commitment. She couldn't stand it. She wanted more from him.

"Don't kiss me again," she said, and pushed him away from her. "I must have been giving you the wrong signals." Her next words tumbled out, "It's not wise behavior." At his raised eyebrows, her hand brushed across her forehead.

"Drat that love potion. It's upset our lives and makes us act emotionally and out of character. That's what's happened."

The indignation faded from Eric's eyes. He gave her a small grin. "You may be right."

Starr hated having him accept her rejection so casually. His next words were further proof he hadn't been affected by the kiss and her protest.

"How about scouting out the new steak house?" he suggested. "It has to be better than the Palace Diner."

The last thing Starr wanted was to go out to eat.

Each morsel would stick in her throat. But she had to cover up her feelings.

"Okay." A bright smile hid the ache in her heart. "We'll give Aunt Maud and Dr. Ted the allotted week. Thank goodness, there are no more bottles."

Looking around Ed's Steak House, Starr agreed with Eric on its merits over the Palace Diner. She had managed to eat half of her sandwich and drink two cups of coffee. She asked Eric about his research, and talked about it through the meal. Then their conversation switched over to the testing.

"What interests me," Eric said, after he took the last bite of his sandwich, "is the variety of our test couples. Imagine your practical, efficient aunt volunteering. The idea of falling in love so simply seems to snag everyone in its net."

"Once the last bottle proves it was one of the best merchandising gimmicks we've seen for a long time, we can get back to reality."

Starr ruthlessly pushed away the thought there would no longer be a reason for her to be with Eric every night. The hair and the testing had brought them together. A few casual kisses and hugs weren't strong enough to tie Eric to her.

After they finished their dinner, Eric drove to New Age. Starr really didn't want to go in and talk about the potion again. How much better it would be to go for a long drive and cuddle up next to Eric—if he loved her . . .

As soon as they entered the store, Glenda told them her decision.

"I wish you'd take the bottles to your lab, Eric," Glenda insisted. "I don't want to be responsible for them anymore." She pushed the box toward him.

"Any developments between Dr. Thorpe and Mrs. Moreland?" Glenda asked.

"He's been too busy to take time out to pursue her. She's still in Paris."

"Thank goodness Aunt Maud volunteered," Starr said, ignoring the feeling of sadness that swept over her because the experiment was ending. "I don't think Glenda should sell the bottles with the original powder in them. You, Eric, can do what you want with the powder as far as I'm concerned—use chemicals, burn it up, or scatter it to the winds."

She gave a suggestion to Glenda. "After Eric takes the powder, you can fill the bottles with sand and sell them. Your customers will love the story. In the past I've bought small vials of professed fairy dust, each a different color and having its own spell."

An embarrassed smile curved her lips. She took

a deep breath and confessed, "I even dabbed Creative Fire, a blend of herbs and powdered gems, on my forehead one day. I needed to come up with a smashing brochure." A flush colored her cheeks. "That time I followed directions—a dab—and it worked."

"Starr, Starr," Eric said, shaking his head from side to side with a smile softening the stern lines bracketing his mouth. "You never fail to amaze me. First, you declare you don't believe in magic. Then you rub fairy dust on your forehead. What a contradiction! What are we to believe about you?"

"That I'm a very ordinary woman who has a bit of the child still in her and the right to change her mind." Starr stopped looking into Eric's mirth-filled eyes. She wanted to believe it was a gentle, loving levity.

"We'll go now, Glenda," Eric said. He picked up the bottle package.

"Good night, you two."

Outside, they stood close together. The night was balmy with stars twinkling in the deep blue sky. The fragrance of the lilacs perfumed the air. The scent made her think of the Astral Industries representative. Glenda had said she wore a hat trimmed with real flowers. Had there been lilacs on it? A straw hat? An unlikely article of apparel; an unlikely salesperson altogether.

Starr broke the silence. "I have a busy day tomorrow. Shall we leave?"

The ringing of the phone pierced Starr's slumber. She burrowed deeper into her pillow, wanting to ignore the noise. Its persistence couldn't be shut out.

"Hello." Her voice was slurred with sleep. She pried open her eyes and looked at the bedside clock: one-thirty.

"Starr, it's me, Glenda. I just had to call you."

"What's wrong? Are you hurt? Where are you? This had better be good. I was having a wonderful dream."

"*My* dream has come true!" Glenda cried. "Steven proposed tonight, and I accepted."

Starr was wide awake in a rush. "What? We left you closing your shop and going home."

"Yes, isn't it wonderful?"

She launched into her story.

Steven had arrived as she was preparing to leave. He'd been furious because the door was unlocked so late at night. He'd shown his concern for her safety by pulling her into his arms and kissing her. What with one thing leading to another, he had confessed his love for her, a love conceived in their early schooldays. His refusal to give her the building permit had been his excuse to see her again and again while he struggled to accept her choice of occupation.

"Oh, I'm the happiest woman on earth!" Glenda took a deep breath. "And I know the love potion had nothing to do with it. Steven has loved me just about forever."

"I'm happy for you. It's so good you didn't need silly magic to make Steven love you." Starr said softly, "No external force is ruling the world of love."

"Amen to that. I'll let you go back to sleep. See you tomorrow."

Up on the third floor Eric couldn't fall asleep. He wanted Starr in his arms. Her suite of rooms was so close and yet so far. On the way home from the store they hadn't talked much. The testing was done. In a short time, they could agree that no love potion resided in any of the bottles. It would confirm Starr's disbelief in magic.

He had the five bottles and their contents to do with as he wished. His first impulse had been to throw the powder away. It had no magical properties. Yet, something stayed his hand. Why be hasty and then regret the action? He'd decide later, after due thought, what to do with it. He had one idea, but—the time had to be right.

Chapter Ten

"I got a wedding invitation from Melanie," Starr said, as soon as Eric met her outside her office the next evening. "Chandler demanded Melanie set an early date. I always thought she needed a man like Chandler to take charge of her life."

Eric drew Starr aside. "Do you need such a man?" With his hands gently enclosing her shoulders, his eyes seemed to bore into her head, as though seeking to learn her innermost thoughts.

Starr took a deep breath and blocked his efforts. She gave a shaky laugh. "Hey, this is the twenty-first century. Women stand on their own feet."

Not for anything would she have Eric know how she pictured him in her dreams. Masterful, taking her up in his muscular arms, carrying her up wide stairs to his love nest, stifling all her protests with a kiss. Forceful on the one hand, yet understanding, warm, and affectionate on the other. Someone not afraid to show his love in tender physical touches.

She wanted an alpha and a beta man rolled into one!

Eric had a long way to go to meet her criteria. Well, maybe not so long a way. He was becoming more relaxed and at ease. The hand clasp and the arm around her shoulders were becoming more frequent. There had been no more kisses. After all, she had told him to back off. Too bad he had listened to her.

"Come on. I want Glenda to give you her news," Starr urged.

"Can't you?"

Starr shook her head. "It's Glenda's story."

"Well!" exclaimed Starr and Eric in unison when they opened the store door.

Steven and Glenda were locked in a close embrace. They didn't hear the bell on the door.

"I guess you don't have to tell me Glenda's news," Eric drawled.

Glenda broke the kiss and looked over Steven's shoulder at her friends. Her face flushed pink. She whispered in Steven's ear. He didn't hurry to turn around, keeping his arm firmly around her. His smile was the smile of a triumphant warrior.

"When did this happen?" Eric asked.

The story was quickly told. Starr hugged Glenda and Eric thumped Steven on the back.

"Without any question, no love potion in Bottle Two," Starr said with satisfaction. She gave a gasp. She put a hand over her mouth, remembering too late that Steven knew nothing about the love potion.

Steven spun Glenda around to face him. "What's Starr talking about? It better not be any of your mumbo-jumbo."

By the time Glenda had uttered four sentences of explanation, Steven was shaking his head from side to side in amazement. He kept shaking it throughout the bizarre story.

"I'm supposed to believe this? Magic? You've got to be making it all up."

When Glenda gave a woeful sniff, he surprised her with a hoot of laughter. He picked her up and twirled her around in a circle. "As I suspected, you're going to make my life very interesting."

He shook his head again. "How intelligent adults—"

"You just wait," Starr prophesied. "Before long

you'll find yourself talking and thinking of the potion as though it were real."

"What do you say we go to the Twilight Bar at the Inn and celebrate Glenda's and Steven's happiness?" Eric suggested.

He linked arms with Starr and started out the door. "No more kissing under these fluorescent lights. Starr and I know the perfect spot to do that on the way."

Hours later, Starr waltzed slowly around her bedroom, wanting Eric's arms holding her tightly against him as he had at the celebration. She dropped her empty arms and crawled into bed.

Her thoughts turned to Steven and Glenda. Theirs was a longstanding love without the help of a love potion. She was so happy for them. She set aside her own pangs of regret that Eric and she hadn't known each other for years, or had fallen in love long ago as her friends had.

Time was proving not a speck of magic was in any of the bottles. Melanie and Chandler? Possibly.

Though she was on record—loud and clear— that she didn't believe in love potions, still . . . A secret part of her longed to be able to use such a thing and make it work!

After all these weeks, Eric wasn't behaving like

a man in love. A few kisses and hand holding were disappointingly friendly. Though he seemed to want to be with her all the time, it didn't give her any hope that it would develop into a deeper relationship. She didn't even know how long he was going to be in Rural Springs.

Depression began to descend on her like a blanket of fog. Her happiness of the evening evaporated. What was wrong with her that men rejected her? Memories of a past heartache sprang to life and tore her apart. It wasn't fair. She had tried so hard to be loving and thoughtful. And it had all been for naught in the past.

Fortunately, with Eric, she hadn't worn her heart on her sleeve. He had no idea she had spun romantic dreams about him. When he left her, she could still retrieve her self-respect.

No, she wasn't going to cry. She had shed her last tear over a man a year ago.

On the brink of sleep, a worm of a doubt drove sleep away. True, Steven and Glenda had fallen in love years ago, but could it be the love potion had been needed to jump-start Steven's declaration of love?

Starr gave a groan and punched her pillow into another shape. Would she ever be free of thoughts about the potion?

*   *   *

Eric went over the day's activities as he lay on his back in bed that night.

Being extra careful, the contents of the crystal bottles had been emptied into a test tube and corked. The small amount of powder he retrieved from five of them surprised him. The crystal walls of the bottles had to be thicker than they looked.

So, he mused, there weren't many pinches that could be thrown. Then why had Starr's bottle contained so much powder? The small amount in one of the bottles wouldn't have covered his head and shoulders. Starr's bottle had been the same size— then why so much powder? Did it expand and grow when it mixed with the air?

Eric frowned. Nothing about this was logical and consistent. When he put the powder in a test tube, the air hadn't affected the amount of it.

He had held the test tube to the light and gently shook it. Nothing happened to change the contents.

Eric took a deep breath. There wasn't enough powder to carry out his fantasy of a beautiful woman's skin gleaming with the magic dust. Ah, the death of a dream.

He'd placed the test tube in the breast pocket of his suit coat and brought it back to the Inn. He didn't want to let it out of his care.

He'd stay in Rural Springs until Astral Industries sent back their salesperson.

It was strange for him to remain in one place all this time. He even found himself content in sleepy Rural Springs. But it wasn't the place that caused him to extend so readily his contract with Bradley Laboratory. A pert young woman with emerald eyes and the bewitchment of a love potion were to blame. No man could fight such a compelling combination of reality and fantasy.

When emptied over his unsuspecting head, the contents of a small crystal bottle had changed his world forever. Actually, the person who had tipped the bottle was responsible for his life becoming interesting and exciting. More than that, he was beginning to suspect that the feeling he found growing each day for his beautiful Starr was of a forever kind.

If that were so, would he be able to persuade her to come with him wherever he had to go? Or was she bound to the place of her birth? He knew she loved Rural Springs with a passion and had been away only during her college years. Her business also chained her to this spot. It was hard for him to understand such attachment to a physical place. His work, which took him to many places, had been the controlling factor in his life.

He got up and prowled around the bedroom, his

troubled thoughts tumbling in his mind. The difference in their personalities was an even greater obstacle to a relationship than where they would live.

Starr was open and affectionate. When he had drawn away from her time and time again, he knew he had disappointed and hurt her. Hadn't he agreed too readily not to kiss her any more? Surely she would view his actions as a lack of affection for her.

Damnation. Feeling the way he did for the first time in his life gave him no precedents to fall back on. He knew he longed to touch her and kiss her senseless every time he came near her. Every minute he was away from her, too.

To his consternation, he realized, for the first time, that he had fallen in love with Starr. To further astound him, it had happened when he looked into her eyes after the powder covered him in a cloud. Literally, love at first sight. And not because of a love potion, either!

Since he now knew he loved Starr and they had finished the testing, he would concentrate on convincing her his love wasn't prompted by magic. Forget the powder—he was going to beg her, on bended knee, if necessary, to teach him how to show his love and affection for her.

*   *   *

"Starr."

She glanced up to see Eric coming toward her in the lobby the next morning. She hadn't expected to see him. As usual, happiness flowed over her like a molten river of lava. Though she knew she was foolish to have her feelings for him grow more and more each day, she still longed to see him all the time. This sight of him would brighten her entire day.

"Good morning," he said.

A simple two-word greeting and oops, there went her temperature. She was becoming a basket case; there wasn't anything she could do to stop it. But she could control her voice and answer him coolly.

"Good morning, Eric."

"It's always a good morning when I see you."

"Thank you for your kind words. I try to please." When she heard the words come out of her mouth, Starr almost groaned. Eric would think she was a throwback to the Victorian Age. Fortunately, she saw he was acting relaxed and at ease with her. It made the moment able to be endured.

Eric took the test tube out of the inside pocket of his coat. He held it up for her to see. "The total amount of powder from five bottles is in this one test tube."

He waited for her reaction.

"That's strange. Especially when my bottle had so much." Then she cried, "No! Please don't tell me we're back to questions without answers."

"Sorry. Can't give you an explanation at this time." He gave her shoulder a comforting squeeze. "I'd appreciate it if you'd take the empty bottles back to Glenda sometime today. I've given them to the reception clerk. I'll be working late tonight."

"Of course. Do you know how late?"

"No, I'll call you." His warm gaze fastened on her mouth, searing her, but he didn't bend his head to kiss her. With a wave of his hand, he was gone.

Starr stood gazing after him until he disappeared out the door. If only he had kissed her! Why was he so different today? His voice so warm? And the look in his eyes. She took a deep breath and savored their brief meeting.

When she walked to her office, she couldn't remember if her feet touched the ground or if she floated there. She did know the sky had never been so blue or the songs of the birds so sweet.

"Starr, what's wrong with you?" Melanie's loud voice startled her. "I've asked you for the third time if you've called the Adams Agency to tell them about their brochure."

"Sorry. Guess I was distracted. Yes, I took care of it." No guess about it. Eric, not business, occupied her thoughts.

An hour later it was Starr who complained. "Melanie, I've asked you to take this brochure to the printer."

"Sorry, Starr. I was thinking of what to serve at our reception."

"We're a pair of scatterbrains today. I think we can blame it on the men in our lives."

"Is it Eric?" Melanie asked, her eyes wide. "Has he asked you to marry him?"

"Oh, no. You're getting ahead of me. We're just friends."

Melanie went back to work, but Starr's thoughts kept on tumbling in her mind. "Friends" was the correct word. She feared it would never deepen. She had to keep remembering this fact and not be going off into dreamland.

She needed to think of something else.

Why the disparity in the amounts of powder? The inside volume in the bottles Eric emptied had to be different from her bottle. That was nothing to worry about: Eric would measure and weigh everything. She'd rely on him to figure it out.

Starr went to the window and looked at her dream catcher. By all rights, it should be hanging over the headboard of her bed, to catch her dreams of Eric. She took it down. Tonight it would be in her bedroom. But she wanted more than dreams. She wanted the real thing—a flesh and blood, virile man, not a phantom of the night.

"You know about Glenda and the mayor?" Melanie's eager voice broke into her thoughts. "I heard about their engagement at the Diner this morning." Her eyes widened with wonder. "To think they've been fighting about that old building permit and covering up their true feelings." Melanie leaned her chin on her hand and looked dreamy-eyed. "Isn't love just wonderful?"

Starr nodded her head in agreement. Love was wonderful . . . but only if two people arrived at that conclusion at the same time.

It was torture if one-sided. Eric and she were two very different people. Sure, opposites did attract, but real life demanded that two lovers have enough in common to live in harmony and contentment. She was more than willing to bend over backwards and compromise if she loved someone. She knew she could make a difference in Eric's life. She'd give him all the love and attention he needed and never begrudge doing it.

Starr stared at her computer screen. She had to stop mooning and get the brochure on Scotland finished.

Oh, to go on that trip to Edinburgh with Eric.

... To have him don a kilt and be her Scottish lord dancing to the lilting music of the bagpipes!

Starr gave a groan. No way was she going to get any work done this morning. She might better go home to the Inn, get the crystal bottles for Glenda, and check on Eric's briefcase.

Its continued disappearance was like a personal affront to her and the Inn. True, it helped to keep Eric in Rural Springs. She knew he wouldn't leave without his important research notes. One way to keep him here would be to hide the briefcase after she found it. An idea, but she was too honest to do that.

She grabbed her purse and headed back to the Inn. On the way, she stopped to talk to friends and neighbors. She realized anew how much she loved living in a small village, a place where everyone knew her and wished her well.

"Starr, Starr," hissed Maud Evans in a loud whisper. She beckoned for her niece to come toward her. Starr had just picked up the potion bottles. Her aunt grabbed her hand. She pulled her down the hall to the swinging double doors to the kitchen.

"Look through the window into the kitchen," she whispered. "Be careful. Don't let them see you."

Chapter Eleven

Starr gasped and pressed her hand over her mouth to smother a cry of surprise.

Allister Kincaid, his white chef's hat sliding down his high forehead, was bending his thin, lanky frame to meet the upturned rosy lips of Millicent Dean. Her hands framed his face and she stood on tiptoe. His arms circled her plump waist as he slowly drew her closer to him.

The embrace and kiss were so tender and sweet that tears filled Starr's eyes. She looked over to her aunt; her eyes were wet, also.

The two women tiptoed away and returned to the lobby, not wanting to spy a moment longer on such a touching and private scene.

"Will wonders never cease?" Maud declared with awe. "Your love potion must have been in Millicent's bottle."

Starr nodded her head. Though she didn't want to believe, she was happy for Millicent and Allister.

Starr felt a little bewildered. What she had just seen meant the love potion had wrought its magic in a definite way. They weren't even expecting to see a positive result. She had doubted it in the case of Melanie and Chandler. But Millicent and Allister were a couple deliberately chosen for the test. Did this mean it might work in their other couples? The thought was unsettling, to say the least. Of course, it might still turn out that only Bottle Four had the potion. She would have to reserve her judgment on the other couples until— until—heavens, she didn't know! Wait and see had to be the case. She knew what the reaction would be tonight at the store.

Deciding not to think about the potion any more, Starr asked, "Any news about Eric's briefcase?"

"I don't understand it at all," Maud said, shaking her head. "We've never lost anyone's luggage. It's almost as if a mysterious force were at work around here lately."

"Please don't say that. I'm having a hard time

keeping a sane head on me without you joining in the general craziness. Did you hear about Glenda and Steven?"

"At least magic didn't cause their engagement." She patted Starr's shoulder affectionately. "A big relief to you, isn't it?"

"Yes. Though after what we just witnessed, we have to suspend our final judgment as to whether the potion will work on some of the other test couples. You included!"

"Are you suggesting I should be encouraged to keep on hoping?"

"Definitely." Starr gave her aunt a hug. "Incidently, since the testing is over, Glenda has given Eric the powder from the five bottles. Surprisingly, there wasn't much in them. I guess that's why the directions said to use only a pinch."

Maud looked closely at Starr. "How are you and Eric getting along?"

"More of the same. Friendly interest only."

"Don't you worry, dear. We both know how dense men can be about what is so good for them."

"Dr. Ted—"

"More of the same, too. But you've raised my expectations."

Starr put her arm around her aunt's shoulder and kissed her cheek. "I should go."

She glanced back toward the kitchen. "Let me know about any further developments. Wasn't that the most touching, heart-tugging kiss you've ever seen? A romance writer should have witnessed it and immortalized it in a book."

"I can hardly wait to talk to Millicent."

"Do you think they'll leave the Inn?"

"Good heavens, I hope not." Maud's hands fluttered to the neck of her dress. "I can't get along without them. They can live in the cottage at the back of the garden. I'll have it redecorated while they're on their honeymoon."

"Whoa! Aren't you getting ahead of yourself? That was probably their first kiss, and you've sent them away on a honeymoon." Starr giggled. "You're one fast worker of miracles."

Maud smiled ruefully. "Perhaps I've become a believer in your magic, for them and for me, too."

"What will be, will be. And that holds for my life also. 'Bye before you and I become maudlin."

"I don't care," Starr muttered to herself as she walked to the New Age Store. She still didn't believe in any old love potion, even after seeing the impossible in the Inn's kitchen. She might concede it could jump-start an existing love, but it could never start a love that wasn't there in the first place.

She kicked a small stone to the side of the walk-way in a fit of frustration. Why did the salesperson leave six bottles of her troublemaking dust? If she had only left the one bottle she had dumped on Eric, there wouldn't be five couples for her to ag-onize over. Was there or wasn't there a magic powder, a bona fide love spell?

At the store, when Starr had finished her story about Millicent and Allister, Glenda smiled broadly. "Her bottle must have had the potion af-ter all. Regardless, it's so sweet when two older people find each other. It makes tears come to my eyes."

"I know how you feel. Here's your five bottles. Eric has the powder from them. Surprisingly, the amount was very small. He can't account for it. Another mystery."

"I'll fill them with sand," Glenda mused.

"Put some color in it. Make up your own bro-chure about its wonderful magic."

Glenda shook her head at Starr. "You do amaze me. One minute you're adamant against the no-tion; the next, you're giving me suggestions on how to merchandise magic charms."

"What can I say? I'm a woman who has to put her two cents into everything."

*   *   *

"I have a few minutes before dinner to tell you Millicent's story." Maud took Starr by the arm and led her into her suite. They settled down in the chintz-covered armchairs.

Starr took a sip of her coffee. "I can't wait to hear this."

"After breakfast Millicent went for a walk. A little brown and white Pekingese dog with a bloody paw was whining in the pathway. Of course, she picked him up and carried him to the Inn. While going through the kitchen, Allister confronted her. He demanded to know what she was doing with his dog. To cut the story short, their mutual concern over Allister's beloved dog destroyed the wall between them, bringing them together. Millicent was so happy, she forgave me that my promised love potion didn't work. She never needed it anyway."

"So a dog's responsible for their love story?"

Starr refilled her cup, adding raspberry cappuccino nonfat creamer this time. "I really wanted the love potion to be in at least one bottle." She confessed to her aunt, "I don't want Eric to leave— ever."

"He's your man?"

"Silly, isn't it? If only he'd take his nose out of his test tubes and see me as a woman instead of an experiment."

Maud looked at her watch. "Have to run. The dinner crowd will be here shortly. Stay and have another cup of coffee." She left the room, only to stick her head back in. "Still checking for that dratted briefcase. No luck!"

Starr settled back in her chair. She stirred her coffee absently.

One by one, they were ruling out the possibility of a love potion being in any of the bottles.

Love had come without it.

Steven and Glenda, high school sweethearts. Melanie and Chandler, the strong man wanting to protect and care for a woman. Millicent and Allister, love for a dog giving them the push toward each other.

She knew Maud and Ted were already in love, long before the potion was thrown. There was even hope for Dr. Thorpe and his Angela. Surely Angela had used the promise of the donation to make certain they saw each other frequently. Hadn't that been the case with Steven?

Eric and herself. She was finally willing to admit it was love for her, but not Eric. Being analytical, scientific, and reasonable had been his behavior from the start of this whole affair. Did a man with those attributes ever just fall in love? Pretty far-fetched.

There would be a logical reason why no one

fell in love when the dust was thrown on them. The polluted air of our earth had killed its potency, or they had waited too long to test it, or . . . or . . . or whatever. So what if it hadn't worked according to the directions?

Yet some of the couples brought in contact with the love potion had their eyes opened to see an existing love.

An existing love.

That was the crux of some of the experiences. Of course, there was no previous existing love in Eric's and her case. Her love dated only from the fateful night when she didn't follow the directions. Was Eric denying truthfully that he hadn't fallen in love with her at the same time—the last gasps of a dyed-in-the-wool bachelor? Hopefully, he'd realize it soon and end her unhappiness.

Starr put down her coffee cup and got up. She heard the hum of voices in the dining room blending with the soft background music. It was time for her to eat another lonely dinner.

Where was Eric eating? In the cafeteria or at his lab table? Probably he had forgotten to eat at all. He needed—a wife! She had to believe and be patient, very patient.

At the lab, Eric made a decision.
He wasn't going to destroy the potion.

Taking a pinch of the powder, he rolled it between his two fingers. What would happen if he convinced Starr to use it as a bath powder? Would she become magically different? Would she glow with an ethereal, heavenly light? Softer to the touch than his wild fantasies? Eric felt himself react with desire.

His contact with the potion made him believe in the unbelievable, ready to become irrational and imaginative. In that way, magic was in those bottles. Yes, the magic . . . the magic of transforming love.

Love.

He had truly fallen in love with Starr—without a by-your-leave. It made him desire to touch her, to kiss her, impatient to be with her again. To laugh with her and talk to her. To protect her. He saw her face behind his eyelids even as he worked.

Had it happened the moment the potion fell on him? Before he looked up? Eric shook his head. The magic powder had nothing to do with it. When he looked up into the laughing eyes of the beautiful woman leaning over the balcony, a miracle occurred.

Because of his ignorance, he hadn't recognized it—not surprising, since he was a stranger of the first water to the emotion called love. Sure, he had read and heard a great deal about it, almost ad nauseam, but that wasn't the same thing as experiencing it.

Eric got up from his stool. He paced restlessly about the lab, thrusting his hands into the pockets of his jacket. Throwing back his head, he gave a loud, happy laugh.

He was in love!

His world, which had tilted several nights ago, was back on its prescribed axis. Since he had identified what was going on in his life, he could plan his strategy to overcome Starr's doubt and distrust.

The failure of their testing was the best thing to happen. No one was relying on magical power to bring about the heady miracle of love in their lives.

He still had the powder. He confessed to himself a niggling belief that, just maybe, it had magical powers. He shook his head. What a pervasive hold the mere thought of a possible unknown power had on the mind of an unbeliever as himself. No matter how hard he tried, he couldn't rid himself of that desire to believe.

His briefcase hadn't turned up. Until its absence was resolved, he'd remain at the Inn and continue working at Bradley Laboratory.

What about the last two couples? Would love

conquer all? He'd encourage John to fly to Paris. Women love to be pursued.

Eric tucked the test tube into the breast pocket of his jacket. He didn't want to leave it in his lab. He wanted to keep it safe on his person until he made a final decision about it.

Chapter Twelve

"Mr. Hammond, Mr. Hammond."

Maud Evans' call stopped Eric as he was going out the door the next evening. He had agreed to meet Starr at the store. Before he answered, he glanced at his wristwatch. Half an hour late already.

"Yes, Miss Evans?"

"Dr. John Thorpe is your supervisor, isn't he? He gave me your name." At Eric's nod, she continued, a small frown furrowing her forehead, "He just called. From Paris, can you imagine? Did you know he was there?"

Eric smiled, "No, but I'm not all that surprised. Mrs. Moreland is there."

154

"Such an unsettling phone call," she complained. "He wants to reserve our best honeymoon suite for sometime next week." She sniffed, "Sometime. Doesn't he realize I have to have specific dates?"

"Great! What good news! So the old boy dashed over to Paris in pursuit of his lady love." Eric smiled down at her. "My advice is to reserve a suite for the whole week. Won't Starr be happy—" He stopped. "Please excuse me, but Starr is waiting for me." He hurried to the door. "Don't worry," he tossed over his shoulder.

Another triumph for love due to the decisive action of a man in love. John had done it on his own without help from magic.

One more couple to go. He whistled as he got into his car. He had no doubts about Maud Evans' ability to accomplish anything, be it running a prestigious hotel or bringing an absent-minded doctor to his senses.

When the last result was in, the testing would be over. No need for even the return of the intriguing salesperson.

When he entered the New Age Store and looked around, Eric's heart swelled with an unfamiliar joy. Three people very dear to him, waited. For the first time in his life he felt at home. Dreary, lonely hotel rooms, in so many places, were not for him anymore. A blueprint of an appealing house he had seen, surfaced in his memory. He could build it on the LOT FOR SALE on the shores of Oteango Lake. A house perfect for a wife and a family.

His position at Bradley was firm. It would be good to stay in one spot instead of trouble-shooting in different medical centers, a stranger in a strange place. With his Aunt Margaret dead, no one in the world cared whether he lived or died. It had never bothered him before, but now, he wanted someone to love him, to share a home with him and have his children.

Starr turned and saw Eric in the doorway. She smiled the smile that brightened his world like ten suns. She waved her hand in greeting.

"Any news for us?" Steven asked. He pulled Glenda closer to his side. "We've come to the conclusion the power of the love potion lies in our minds only."

"It does look that way," Eric agreed. "I have great news."

There was a hubbub of surprise and happiness.

"The indefinite request for a reservation in the middle of our busiest period won't be easy for Aunt Maud to arrange," Starr commented.

"Will she be able to do it?" Eric asked.

"She'll try her best, I'm sure," Starr answered. "She's accomplished some miracles through the years. She says it all turns out well because Cupid is on her side." She gave a little laugh. "Do you think love came to Rural Springs this summer because we already had an established history of helping lovers?"

"Makes good sense," Glenda mused. "Any developments in your aunt's love life?"

"Not yet." Starr smiled ruefully. "Though surrounded by lovers for years, Aunt Maud has been untouched by Cupid's arrow. When she realized this, she used the love potion in desperation. She still hopes Dr. Ted will awake from his slumber and pop the question."

"What can we do to help things along?" Steven asked.

"Please, nothing!" Starr's answer was decisive. "Love has to be equally strong for both individuals or you'll have an unhappy ending. Let them work things out by themselves." She took a deep breath. "Like most people, I don't want interference in my life, magical or otherwise. I'm as pleased as I can be because an existing love has surfaced recently in the lives of some of our test couples." She turned to Glenda and Steven. "Isn't that true for you?"

Steven gave Glenda a quick kiss before he nodded his head.

Starr looked at Eric from beneath her thick lashes. She wondered if he had been affected by this talk of love—of love, maybe, for her? Everyone around her seemed to be in love. Why not Eric and she? She looked closely at Eric as he talked with Steven, and shook her head.

He looked the same—calm, quiet, and controlled. No earth-shaking emotion of love changed his demeanor.

Not wanting to join the others, Starr walked to the shelves with the silver figurines. Picking up the one of Merlin, she marveled at the ability of the artist to portray the wisdom in the wizard's face as he looked into the trusting eyes of his pupil Arthur. If only she could sit at a wise man's feet and get the answers to her questions or be instructed on how to react to the frustrating, aggravating love of her life.

"Hey, Starr, what's with the antisocial act tonight?" Eric asked. He walked over and drew her back to the others. "Since you suggested it, what color sand should be put in the crystal bottles?"

"Bright, cheery hues. To make people happy. The yellow of the daffodil, the blue of the summer sky, the violet found in our lilacs, the new green of the spring foliage, and the pink of a heavenly rose."

"Perfect," Glenda agreed. "How about becoming my partner? I need your imagination."

"Oh, no, not me. This is how I paint a picture of each trip in my brochures. The colorful words make it difficult for the customer to resist the allure of 'faraway places, with the strange-sounding names.' "

"Which trip would you go on if you could leave in a couple of weeks?" Eric asked.

"Oh, my," Starr laughed. "I'm so fickle. I fall in love with whatever country I'm working on. Right now, it's Scotland. Heaven only knows what it will be in a couple of weeks." She turned to Eric. "Ask me later."

Eric smiled at her. "I will. You can bet on it."

Starr stared at him in confusion. The interplay between them had suddenly become charged. Why was he asking about her preference in travel plans? She wanted it to mean what she desired more than anything—to share a honeymoon with him.

"Heavens, look at the time. Will you drive me back to the Inn, Eric?"

"My chariot awaits, my fair maiden," Eric said. He bowed and doffed an imaginary hat.

Starr's laughter filled the air. Securing her seatbelt, Starr congratulated herself for not revealing her turbulent thoughts. She must never let Eric know her true feelings for him.

Starr looked up from the Inn's accounts she was working on in the cozy Inn office the next morning.

Happiness radiated from her aunt. Without a word, she held out her left hand. A square-cut diamond with emerald stones on either side sparkled on her third finger.

Starr shot out of her chair and hugged her aunt. "You're engaged! Tell me all about it."

Maud gave a shaky laugh and wiped the sudden tears from her eyes.

"It happened as I always dreamed it would—last night, under the spell of the new moon. Ted declared his undying love for me and asked for my hand in marriage. Starr, he was so sweet. I think he would have gone down on bended knee if I had been seated. But we were walking down the street. He stopped me by those tall lilac bushes. His words just tumbled out as though he was afraid he'd lose his courage. And then we—well, never mind." Her cheeks turned a rosy pink.

Starr gave her another hug and kissed her cheek. "I'm so happy for you both. What are your plans, or haven't you thought that far ahead?"

Maud fluttered about the office, picking up objects and putting them down again. "We have a problem," she confessed.

"Anything I can do?" Starr took Maud's hands in hers.

"Ted wants us to marry at the end of the week. He has a medical conference in Vienna in seven days. We could go there as part of our honeymoon."

"And you're worried about leaving the Inn in the middle of the season." Starr looked into the troubled eyes of her aunt. "No problem, dear heart. You know how efficient Charlie James is as your second-in-command. He'll be delighted to prove his worth. I'll be here if family business comes up. Let's get busy on your wedding right away. I just love this!"

"I'll leave everything to you. Ted will be so happy when I call him." A quick embrace and she was gone.

As Starr made phone calls and arranged for a small family wedding, she had to bury the depression that threatened to overtake her. All the people around her had fallen in love and were planning for "forever after."

Five weddings.

Her Aunt Maud's was to be the first, closely followed by the others. The domino theory in real life. She could have the dubious honor of being "always a bridesmaid, never a bride" at this rate.

Eric wasn't in love with her.

Since she was the one who started all the events, it was ironic. By all rights, Eric and she should have been the first couple to declare their love and plan the first wedding.

Starr gave herself a shake. She wouldn't give in to her dark thoughts. No more self-pity—life goes on. She would continue with all the courage she could muster. She'd paint on a happy face and laugh and smile. No one would ever be the wiser—especially Eric.

That evening, in the back room of the New Age Store, they celebrated the end of the testing. Steven brought a bottle of Champagne. Signs of the Zodiac circled the dark blue ice bucket. The Champagne was served in Glenda's best star-studded crystal goblets.

They toasted each couple.

After the last toast, Starr said, "What an interesting time we've had since Glenda bought the potion. We've pretty much established that it didn't work immediately or as we thought it should. However, our five subjects are in love. Maybe the magic did work. We can't discount its power completely, that's for sure." She turned to Eric. "You're the scientist—what is your verdict?"

"The same as yours. All I can say is that someone or something set the wheels in motion for love to have a working holiday in Rural Springs." Eric looked intently at Starr and a smile lurked at the corners of his mouth. "*Five* bottles and *five* couples. Each had their own experience because of exposure to the potion."

Starr stared at Eric. He had emphasized the five. From the beginning he'd said he hadn't fallen in love because of the love potion. He had ruled out the first bottle. Time had proven him right. No longer was she going to bat her head against the stone wall of his indifference.

She turned her back on Eric and spoke to Glenda.

"I'm depending on you to help me decorate the church, Glenda."

"Sure thing. I have just the right streamers—"

"Oh, no. You're going to need supervision."

"Starr, wonderful news!"

Starr closed the lobby door. She turned to see her aunt waving a letter. "Mr. and Mrs. James Thatcher have Eric's briefcase." She unfolded the letter. "They just arrived home from a side trip to their daughter, who had gone into premature labor with their first grandson. Naturally, everything was all sixes and sevens. They finally got back to Phoenix. It was then they found Eric's briefcase, which had somehow been forwarded with their other luggage."

"How marvelous. Have you told Eric?"

"No, the letter only came a few minutes ago. I saw him leave over an hour ago."

"I'll call him," Starr said. "Better yet, I'll drive out to the lab." Starr turned back from the door. "Did the Thatchers say when they're sending the briefcase?"

Maud read further down the letter. "They've already mailed it Priority Mail. It should be here soon."

"I'm on my way. Such good news should be delivered in person. Hope we have no more trouble. Eric has been remarkably patient."

"He's a very fine young man and I admire him." Maud gave a sly little laugh. "Of course, not as much as you do. And you can't deny it."

Starr felt a blush working its way from her neck up into her cheeks. From childhood, she hadn't been able to hide her feelings. She had been teased and taunted because of it. She didn't answer her aunt, giving only a wave as she went out the door, walking quickly to the parking lot.

After she reached the parking lot of Bradley

Laboratory, Starr sat in her car. She took several deep breaths and wiped the perspiration from the palms of her hands. Out of the clear, she had a premonition of doom. Well, not quite doom, but a feeling she was going to hear something unpleasant. It shouldn't be happening this morning. She was the bearer of good tidings.

She asked the receptionist to page Eric.

Starr watched Eric as he strode quickly down the long corridor toward her. She noticed immediately a difference about him. His step was light, and he was all smiles.

A premonition again filled her. For a moment, she thought of running away, out the door and back to her friendly, homey office.

"What a pleasant surprise," he said, as he grasped her two hands and squeezed them gently. The excitement that was vibrating in him flowed into her, setting every nerve on alert. "Your visit will truly make my day."

"We've located your briefcase," she blurted out.

"More good news." Eric's smile became broader.

Starr explained about the Thatchers.

"That takes a load off my mind. Now, more than ever, I'm glad to have it back." Eric asked, "Can you stay for a few minutes? I want you to be the first to hear my news." He urged her to sit down and sat across from her. He pulled a crumpled letter from his pocket. He smiled fatuously at her.

"I've been offered a full fellowship at the California Research Institute."

At Starr's blank look, he laughed. "It's outside San Diego and is the best endowed research center in the United States. No money worries there as we have here." He explained, "It's the ideal center for cancer research. They want me. Isn't that great?"

Eric's eyes sparkled and his smile couldn't get any broader. He sprang from his chair as though he couldn't sit still. He looked expectantly at her.

No, no, no, Starr cried silently with every fiber of her being. Eric was going to leave her. She called upon every inner resource of courage to react as he wanted her to do.

"How simply wonderful! You must answer them immediately. Will you leave soon?" She babbled, "How fortunate we've located your briefcase, so there's nothing to keep you. Even our silly testing of the love potion is finished."

Glancing at her wristwatch, she cried, "I must run or I'll be late for my appointment. See you—sometime."

Without looking at Eric, she turned and quickly left the building.

Eric stared after her, bewildered and hurt. Why had she run away? He had been so happy to see her. Sure, his news was exciting, but it didn't hold a candle to his joy at her unexpected appearance.

The offer from California had been a surprise. Since he had tendered it last year, he never expected to be accepted. Had it come at that time, there was no doubt he would have accepted it. However, he was happy here at Bradley and more content than he'd ever been to be living in a small town. He'd made friends. Most important of all, he had found the only woman who could make him happy all the days of his life.

He thrust his hands into the pockets of his trousers. His eyebrows drew into a deep frown as he recalled the scene of a few minutes ago.

Starr wanted him to leave as soon as possible.

He felt as though she had dealt him a blow to the solar plexus. Had he been misreading her body language and the look in her eyes all these weeks? It didn't seem possible he had been so off base. Since he came to the Inn, surely she had sought him out every night—hadn't she?

He gave a short laugh. Of course, all she had wanted was to absolve her aunt's Inn of any responsibility for the hair fiasco.

He read the letter again. A year ago it would have been the crown to his career. Anger began to burn within. Starr should have acted differently on hearing his fabulous news. Sure she should have been glad for him, but she also should have showed sadness and dismay that he might be leaving.

She should have waited long enough for him to explain he was going to reject the offer. Why had she run away in such a huff?

He folded the letter and put it into his pocket. Tomorrow would be time enough to accept the offer. With Starr acting in such an uninterested manner, there was nothing to keep him in Rural Springs. The sooner he left the better. However, only after he wrapped up his work at the lab and attended Maud's wedding.

He was thankful John was still in Paris. He couldn't persuade him to stay.

It was fortunate the phase he had been working on at work was near completion. A few more days and he could wind up his research.

He'd leave his heart behind him.

The earlier spring in his step was gone. His shoes shuffled on the tile as he slowly walked back to his lab.

Starr kept a tight rein on her emotions. Her shoulders were thrown back and her head held high as she walked with a steady pace to her car.

She longed to have Eric call her back, to tell her she was wrong in assuming he wanted to go to California. Silence followed her.

Her seatbelt in place, she pulled out of the parking lot. She forced herself to drive at a moderate speed along the highway. At the crossroads, she turned to the right, taking the scenic road that wound around the shores of Oteango Lake. She passed the sign LOT FOR SALE, at the location of her dream house. Five miles from town, she parked at one of the pleasant turnouts.

Only then did she relax her tight hold of the steering wheel. Releasing the seatbelt, she folded her arms over the wheel and dropped her head on them. Tears flowed down her cheeks, and her shoulders heaved with her sobs.

Eric was leaving.

Her heart was a hard lump in her chest, and each breath was painful. Although she had been subconsciously expecting it, this blow had come so quickly. Her world had been turned upside down in a few minutes.

She sat up straight and threw back her head.

The best thing for her to do today was to get back to work. She also needed to check if Eric's briefcase had arrived—to tie up that one loose thread, anyway. Its location had come at the right time.

A tiny worm of doubt inched its way up her spine.

The right time.

Were strange forces at work? So many events were suddenly happening. So many loves had been discovered, almost like the pieces of a jigsaw puzzle falling into place. Did an unseen hand—Fate—put them there?

Starr resolved to stop her unproductive moaning and groaning. She made up her mind to be happy for Eric. How fortunate she hadn't made a fool of herself by revealing she loved him.

Eric was a wanderer, never putting down roots. His work was his life. Love had no power over these damning facts. As though a leopard could change his spots.

Foolish Starr, foolish, foolish Starr!

The testing of the love potion had provided him with entertainment and relaxation from his serious research work. She had been a part of that package, easily discarded and probably easily forgotten, too. Enough.

She wiped the tears from her cheeks. Crying was getting her nowhere. This wasn't the end of her world, by a long shot. Anyway, she had her dear aunt's wedding to plan. It would be the best one ever seen in Rural Springs because of her planning.

Chapter Thirteen

Seven days later, the afternoon of the wedding was beautiful with bright sunshine and a playful breeze. The lilacs filled the air with their spicy fragrance. The daffodils, impatiens, petunias, and geraniums were at the peak of their beauty.

The ceremony was to be held at four o'clock in the historic, vine-covered family church.

An hour before the service, Starr and Glenda were making the finishing touches.

"For the last time, Glenda, we aren't going to have Zodiac trimmed bows on the ends of the pews." Starr's voice was firm. "We're going to have white, plain white satin bows with lilies of the valley in the center. As Aunt Maud requested."

Starr wondered if it had been a mistake to ask Glenda, always full of her New Age ideas, to help her decorate the church. Yet, she would never have gotten the wedding plans carried out without her. She gave Glenda a quick hug.

Starr looked up the aisle to the door of the church. Next, her gaze flicked over the entire room. Traditional, with a touch of the Victorian, was the theme. The bouquets of white and purple lilacs, with their ruffle of lace, were in place, their fragrance permeating the old stone church. In a few hours the bride would come down to stand before the old carved altar. There she'd make her vows to the man of her heart.

Every aspect of the wedding week bore Starr's imprint. Even a surprise bridal shower had been squeezed in. She was determined that Maud would have shower gifts to remind her of this momentous day as the years rolled by.

All this hectic activity left little time for her to think about Eric—except in the wee hours of the night when she stifled her sobs. Glenda's overt questions about the fellowship received short replies expressing Starr's happiness for his good fortune.

Eric stayed in the background, taking no part in the preparations.

At no time had he tried to talk to her as she

hurried by. This had really hurt. It was as though the magic dust hadn't been tipped on top of his head or the testing been conducted. The kisses—well, gone down the drain with everything else. She didn't even know when his letter of acceptance was mailed. The puzzling thing was he made no attempt to terminate his stay at the Inn. What was he waiting for? For the return of his supervisor with his new bride on his arm? She wasn't about to question him, to let him think she was interested in his plans to leave.

Starr was to be the maid of honor. Her gown, a pale pink confection of lace and gauze, had rows of ruffles in the skirt. At first she had protested it was too frilly for her. Maud insisted otherwise. However, the more she looked at it, the better Starr liked it. She wondered if Eric would, too.

Ted's nephew was to be the best man. He was a good head shorter than she. The Mutt and Jeff title suited them.

A cousin was to be the little flower girl. Susan had begged for the privilege. "Please, please, please. I've always wanted to throw petals before the bride. This could be my only time to do it." It could be because Starr didn't envision herself as ever getting married. Bitterness and unhappiness formed a big lump in her throat.

"Starr." Ted was hurrying down the aisle. "Last-minute complication."

"No," Starr wailed. "I knew everything was going too smoothly. What is it?"

"My nephew has been taken to the hospital for an emergency appendectomy. Do you think Eric would fill in for him? Your aunt suggested him. If you were to ask him . . ."

Starr's heart began to quicken its beat. Wild hope uncurled and leaped into life in the pit of her stomach. What would it be like to have Eric in the wedding party, to be next to him all day, to have his magnetism reach out and draw her closer to his side? Vivid pictures of her fantasy wedding flashed against her eyelids.

"Of course. I don't know if he has a tux."

"No matter. A suit will do. Everyone will understand."

With another look around the church to make sure everything was in order, Starr hurried out with Ted.

"If you don't hear otherwise, Eric will be your best man. I'll go and reassure my aunt. She must be a bundle of nerves."

"I know—I'm tied up in knots. Do you think all bridegrooms are like me?"

"So I've heard." Starr patted him on the shoulder. "My bets are on you."

* * *

When Starr approached Eric about his new role in the wedding, his eyebrows shot up. "Me? Sure, never expected this honor. I like Ted. Fortunately, I have a tuxedo for the occasion. Will I have a chance to practice?"

"No time for that. All you have to do is stand next to the groom and hand him the ring."

"Guess any fool can do that."

"You're no fool!" Starr protested. His blue eyes were boring into her, as though he was trying to read her inner thoughts.

"Am I anyone else's best man besides Ted's?" he asked softly.

Yes, mine, Starr wanted to shout, but fear of making a fool of herself paralyzed her. Somehow she kept her head from nodding.

"I wouldn't know, Eric. Why don't you ask around?"

Eric gave a soft chuckle and turned away.

The church was filled with well-wishing friends and family. The organist began the stately wedding march, and the chords swelled in volume and filled the sanctuary.

Susan tripped happily down the aisle, throwing her rose petals with enthusiasm, a wide smile wreathing her cherubic face.

When Starr slowly did the hesitation step to the altar, Eric's eyes were fixed on her. Never had she seemed more lovely than she did today. The ruffles of her pink gown swept the floor and her rose bouquet was encircled with white lace. A wreath of baby's breath and rosebuds sat lightly on her golden head. Eric was reminded of a Victorian valentine he had seen in an old shop.

She raised her gaze to his and his world stood still. When her tawny lashes dropped over her eyes, he began breathing again as she continued down the aisle.

During the traditional ceremony, he silently made the same promises . . . in sickness and in health, for richer or poorer, till death do us part. Ted's nudge brought him back to the present ceremony. He quickly fished the rings from his pocket.

"I now pronounce you husband and wife. You may kiss your bride, Ted."

Eric watched as Ted lifted the veil and looked into the radiant face of his bride. The love that flowed between them was almost palpable. His heart was touched to see the union between the two lovers sealed with a kiss. His sigh joined the one rippling over the church.

Before Starr lowered her gaze, Eric saw the tender light in them. He hoped she had been as moved as he had been with the ceremony. Had she also repeated the words as he had? Was it possible they were in perfect accord for once?

The organ broke into the lively tune of the recessional.

Eric held out his arm to Starr so they could follow the bridal pair. He put his hand over hers and pulled her closer to his side. She looked up at him and he was swamped by a surge of deep and abiding love for her.

Since their eyes were only on each other, Eric marveled that they were able to walk down the church steps without falling.

The reception was held on the Inn's grounds. Starr walked under the long blue marquee crowded with buffet tables almost bowed because of the delicious platters of food. For the first time in her memory, Allister Kincaid was all smiles as he supervised the serving of his favorite dishes. Millicent flitted among the guests, making sure all were satisfied. Starr, seeing her blow a shy kiss to Allister when she thought no one was looking, felt choked up with emotion. Such love was beautiful to behold.

She saw that Glenda, who was at the buffet for another helping, was bewildered at the charming smile Allister favored her with. Then she glanced over her shoulder and just caught the end of Millicent's kiss. When Glenda smiled knowingly at her, Starr nodded her head.

When the bridal couple emerged from the front door of the Inn a short time later, there was a shout. Their hopes of a quiet departure were denied. More birdseed and petals showered them as they laughingly got into the car. They left with the tin cans and old shoes dragging behind. A JUST MARRIED sign was on the back of the car.

The party continued after the happy couple departed. When dusk deepened into night, the dragging feet and wide yawns of the youngsters signaled the end of the festivities.

As he had been the entire afternoon, Eric was glued to Starr's side. They ambled toward the patio entrance and watched the exodus. He gave a low chuckle.

"I'll bet you were beginning to think they were going to make an all-nighter of this reception. Everyone seemed to have a good time, didn't they? I know I did."

Though she knew she was being foolish, Starr leaned her head against his shoulder. She was blissfully tired, but she didn't want the day to end.

"I'd like to say, 'I could have danced all night,' as Eliza did in *My Fair Lady*, but I know my body would refuse to act upon my words."

"Are you telling me it's time for Cinderella to leave the ball?"

"Not really."

Eric looked around the patio. They were alone. The silence of the beautiful, still night enveloped them in a cocoon of privacy perfumed with the scent of the flowers. The world seemed far away. At this moment, on this night, Eric felt he could easily believe in the power of magic to lead them into a world of enchantment.

"Stay just a little longer," he begged. He led her to a stone bench. "Please, sit with me. Did I tell you how lovely you look in that gown?"

"Only a half a dozen times," Starr laughed. "Aunt Maud chose the gown over my protests. I like things straight and simple."

"For this fairytale wedding, you had to dress the part." Eric stood up and held out his arms, wanting her close to him.

"Dance with me."

"There's no music."

"Didn't you say the music from *My Fair Lady* was humming through your head? I can hear it, too."

Starr went into his arms and laid her head against his heart. She closed her eyes and enjoyed the closeness.

They circled the patio several times before Eric stopped the dance.

"Starr."

She tipped her head back and looked at his face. Her eyes narrowed as she tried to read the meaning in his smile.

With his gaze holding her captive, he took the test tube out of his breast pocket. His thumb uncorked it. As though held in a spell, she saw him hold it high above her. Slowly the contents cascaded over her like a waterfall.

The small amount of powder seemed to increase magically in volume until they were both enveloped in a shimmering cloud.

Eric lifted Starr off her feet and whirled around and around the patio. They laughed and hugged and kissed amid the snowstorm. When their wild dance slowed down, Eric nestled Starr against him. He smoothed her hair away from her face. An aura of silver light seemed to surround Starr. He had the awesome feeling she was ethereal, not of this world. No wonder the directions instructed only a pinch. Mere mortals were transformed by its magical contents.

Eric gave his head a shake. He was being ridiculous. The magic was of his own imaginative making. The powder enhanced Starr's loveliness, but she was still a woman of this earth and not a creature from other realms.

"Eric."

"Yes?"

"Why did you pour the rest of the love potion on me?"

The smile on his mouth possessed hers in a kiss. She lost all track of time and space.

When the kiss ended and before the second could begin, he murmured, "To be honest, I wanted to throw only a pinch as we've been doing with the others. But, I couldn't resist doing what you did to me. It brought the story full circle. When it happened to me, you declared you didn't believe in its powers. I, too, don't believe. But I had the sudden urge to cover all bases, and found myself pouring all of it on you. Whether there was a love potion I can't prove or disprove." Eric framed Starr's face with his hands. "This one thing I know. I love you. I love you for yourself alone."

Starr's eyes glistened with sudden tears. "Oh, Eric, I love you, love you for yourself alone, too!" Before his lips sought hers, she started to say, "The love potion—"

"Not now, my love."

"Umm . . ."

Later, Starr asked in a dreamy voice, "When did you fall in love with me?"

"Though I didn't know it at the time, it happened the moment I looked up after the powder fell on me. You were trying to hide your laughter to save my feelings. Golden hair and green eyes called to me. In an instant—I was in love."

"You don't think it was this love potion that still covers us? I did throw more than the prescribed pinch!"

"Believe me. The accident only directed my eyes to the woman of my dreams. It had no other function. How can I prove it to you so you will never doubt my love?"

Starr smiled and lifted up her lips. Her arms wound around his neck and her fingers tangled into his hair.

"Kiss me."

After such a command had been fulfilled, Eric asked, "And when did you fall in love with me?"

"When you appeared in the doorway of your room, your hair shining in the light. You became my Prince Charming from my favorite childhood story." Her fingers slipped up the side of his head, "Tell me you love me, Your Highness!"

"I love you, my bright and precious Starr."

Starr gave a little shiver and nestled closer in Eric's embrace. "Oh, darling, this is all so weird.

I don't know what to think. I wonder if supernatural forces have been here in Rural Springs."

Eric kissed her eyes, her cheeks, and, finally, her waiting lips. "Don't be afraid, my dear heart. If it's so, we know the forces aren't going to hurt us in any way. In fact, we've had a rash of love affairs and many happy couples since our little salesperson darkened Glenda's door. For this, I'm very grateful."

They looked at each other and then up into the star-filled sky. Almost of the same mind, they began to laugh.

"I have this strange feeling that magic just might be surrounding us."

"So do I. Crazy, isn't it?"

Starr was silent, savoring being in Eric's arms, with his lips trailing tiny kisses over her cheeks to reach her lips. Drawing back to kiss her again, Eric noticed when a frown appeared on her smooth forehead. Sudden anxiety underlined his question. "What's wrong? What do I have to do to convince you I love you?" He gave a relieved laugh. "I know. I haven't asked the all-important question. Will you marry me and make me the happiest man on earth?"

"Yes, yes, yes!" Her response had to be sealed with another kiss. Then Starr cried, "But you're leaving and going to California."

Eric gathered her close to him. "No, I'm not. I'm staying right here. You didn't wait for me to tell you so when you came to the lab. You practically pushed me to leave as soon as possible. You broke my heart. Then you got all wrapped up in the wedding, having no time or eyes for me."

"Oh, Eric darling, I could have saved myself hours and days of agony and suffering! If I act so headstrong in the future, you'll have to be patient with me."

Eric's kiss was answer enough until he again sensed all wasn't perfect between them.

"Come on, my love, you still have doubts. What are they so I can clear everything up?"

"I don't want to give up my business."

"Why should you? Did I ask you to do so?"

"You said in no uncertain terms you wanted a wife who would stay at home and devote all her time to you and the family."

Eric gave a loud hoot of laughter. "So I did. Forget those foolish words. I only want your happiness. If keeping your business is what you want, it's fine with me. Besides, you have to make travel plans for our honeymoon in Scotland."

Starr's delighted laugh filled the air. "Oh, yes, you remembered!"

His arms around her were tight bands. Her soft

curves fitted with his hard muscles as though poured there. The beat of his heart made her feel warm all over as every nerve tingled and sang. He kissed her with growing passion, teaching her to trust him with her happiness.

Afterward, she said, "Too bad we can't contact Astral Industries to tell them their salesperson doesn't need to come back."

"No, I want to meet her and thank her for my happiness. Without the powder falling on me, I would have stepped onto the patio and gone back in, never knowing you were on the balcony above me. Without the testing of the love potion, I would have left Bradley Laboratory at the end of my original contract."

He held her more tightly, kissing her more ardently.

"Ah, my love, my own special Starr, I shudder to think how easily I might never have fallen in love with you."

"Hold me tight, always," Starr urged. "Never let me go."

"An easy and forever-after command for me to fulfill," Eric promised. His lips found hers to seal his pledge. "We've learned love had its own magic. It doesn't need the aid of any other magic."

Or does it?

DATE DUE

FEB 7 '01			
DVM			

F
BUR   Burton, Ludima Gus

       The love potion

Charlotte County Library
P.O. Box 788
Charlotte C.H., VA 23923